Judith W

The Price o

CW00470960

Table of Contents

I have risen to the pinnacle of power in the Diablo, but my ambitions don't end here. My next move is to claim her as mine, no matter the cost. I would strike a deal with the devil himself to own her.

Born into this world of darkness as a female, I know the rules and expectations. So, when fate dictates that I must marry the leader of the Russian mafia to forge an alliance, I comply, even as my heart rebels.

Together, we navigate treacherous paths and wage war against time, our own limitations, and the encroaching darkness within our organization. Will we conquer the shadows that threaten our love and emerge triumphant? Or will we lose everything we hold dear in this treacherous game of power?

Chapter 1

Kirill

I pace back and forth in my office, consumed by the weight of today's events.

My father's funeral.

The bastard has returned to his home.

I kept my hatred to myself and accepted the condolences without displaying any emotion. Oh, God! How I despise those false words and fake tears.

The events of the day weigh heavily on my mind as I cast my gaze across the vast expanse of my mahogany desk, cluttered with papers and folders. A framed photograph of my late father catches my attention, serving as a constant reminder of the legacy I carry on. His stern gaze seems to pierce through the glass, a silent testament to the path I have chosen and the sacrifices I have made to become the feared and respected leader of the Diabol organization.

The ticking of the clock on the wall reminds me of the impending meeting with my inner circle, my trusted and not-so-trusted Underbosses and Captains who have pledged unwavering loyalty to the organization.

They are my people now, I remind myself.

With each passing second, I draw closer to my goal—the culmination of years of careful planning and calculated moves.

But it's more than just power and control that drives me.

It's a hunger, an insatiable thirst for dominance that burns within me. The weight of the world rests on my shoulders, and amidst the chaos and violence that define our existence, I find a strange solace. I've waited a long time for this moment, for the pieces of the puzzle to align in perfect harmony.

A surge of adrenaline courses through my veins. The anticipation, the knowledge that I am on the cusp of a new era, sends a shiver down my spine. The room is filled with the scent of the coffee I just drank, mingling with the faint aroma of leather and cigar smoke. It's an intoxicating cocktail, a potent elixir that fuels my every move.

I straighten my tie, a symbol of authority and control, and adjust the cufflinks adorning my wrists. Every detail must be immaculate, reflecting the image of a man who demands respect and commands attention. This is my world, and I will stop at nothing to shape it according to my will.

Natasha, my childhood friend and trusted confidante, enters the room with a purposeful stride. Her long black hair falls in sleek waves, cascading over her shoulders like a dark waterfall, accentuating her commanding presence. Her sharp features, sculpted by determination and resilience, convey a sense of unwavering strength. As her steel-gray eyes meet mine, a flicker of understanding passes between us, unspoken words of shared experiences and the unbreakable bond we have forged. From our tumultuous childhood, where we navigated the treacherous waters of our fathers' cruelty, she emerged as a survivor, honing her skills and transforming herself into a valuable asset. She is the mastermind behind the intricate web of information that fuels our operations, her knowledge of the digital realm an invaluable weapon in our arsenal. In a world where secrets hold power, she has become a guardian of our own, ensuring that our vulnerabilities remain hidden from prying eyes.

But there is more to Natasha than her skills and intelligence. Beneath her steely exterior lies a woman who has known pain and hardship, yet refuses to be defined by them. She is a survivor, a warrior in her own right, and her presence is a constant reminder of the strength that lies within us all.

"You seem troubled, Kirill," Natasha observes, her voice filled with concern. "What's weighing on your mind?"

I sigh, as I lean against the desk, my gaze fixes on the skyline outside, surveying the city that has become my playground. "The past, Natasha. It always seems to haunt me," I reply coolly, not betraying any emotion as I continue to gaze out the full-length windows.

My demeanor is practiced and calculated; ever since I was a child, I have learned to keep my feelings buried deep within myself.

In a world where every weakness can be exploited, vulnerability is a luxury I can't afford. "But we can't afford to dwell on it now. And here is Jurij's case," I reply, and I can't help my tone is frustrated. I only show this in front of Natasha, I trust her. "He thinks I have nothing more important to do than listen to his empty ramblings."

Natasha raises an eyebrow. "What does he want now?"

"He's been pressuring me to name him as my Consigliere," I explain. "But I refuse to let his archaic views hinder our progress. I choose you, Natasha, for your skills and dedication. You've earned your place by my side."

Natasha smiles, a mixture of gratitude and determination in her eyes. "Thank you, Kirill. I won't let you down."

"I know."

The next moment the door swings open, revealing Jurij's imposing figure. He exudes an aura of authority, his gray hair slicked back and his eyes sharp with conviction. Jurij has been my father's Consigliere, and he clings fiercely to the traditional values of the old guard.

"Kirill," Jurij greets me, his voice tinged with false respect. "I trust you're considering my request for the position?"

My jaw clenches. "Jurij, I've made my decision. Natasha will serve as my Consigliere. She has proven her loyalty and skills time and again."

Jurij's face twists into a sneer. "A woman as an adviser? This is insane! A woman's place is at home, serving her man and providing pleasure. How can you allow such an abomination within our ranks?"

Natasha's eyes flash with anger, her voice sharp as she steps forward. "My gender doesn't define my worth, Jurij. I've earned my position through hard work and dedication, just as Kirill has earned his place as our Pakhan. We are a modern organization, ready to adapt and thrive in a changing world."

"Jurij, I don't want to hear you talk to her like that again," I declare. "However I respect the contributions you made under my father's leadership, but times are changing, and our organization must change with it. Natasha is more than capable, and I trust her implicitly." I emphasize the word trust.

Jurij's face contorts with a mix of disdain and grudging respect. "Very well, Kirill. I may not agree with your decision, but I will follow your lead. Just remember, the old ways are not to be dismissed so easily."

With those words, he sits down at the far end of the table. I lock eyes with Natasha, and a silent understanding passes between us.

More people arrive and take a seat at the table. The dimly lit room is filled with whispers and uneasy glances, as the members of my organization wait for me to begin the meeting. There is a palpable tension in the air – a mix of fear and respect for me.

When I loudly pull out my chair, the room falls silent immediately, every eye fixes on me.

"Good evening, gentlemen," I nod. "It seems we're all eager to discuss the future of our organization. And I'm sure many of you are wondering what this alliance with Luke and the La Morte means for us."

Several of the men shift uncomfortably, avoiding eye contact with me. I watch them with unyielding intensity. Not everyone will like the direction Diabol is going to take, but will anyone have the guts to speak out? I hope so.

"Allow me to put your minds at ease," I say, and with a smirk, I stand up commanding their full attention. "This alliance isn't about casting anyone aside or usurping power. It's about joining forces for a common goal: to expand our reach, eliminate our enemies, and ensure that we maintain control."

Relief washes over some of the men's faces, but I know better than to trust it entirely. In this world, loyalty is a fragile and fleeting thing.

As I continue discussing my plans for the future, I remain vigilant, aware that each word spoken in this room can be a double-edged sword.

After everyone leaves, Natasha emerges from the corner.

"You don't have to hide," I lean back in my chair.

"I know, I'm just giving them time to get used to the idea that women can hold positions."

"How very generous of you," I tease.

Natasha flashes her eyes and then shrugs. "I grew up in this world, Kirill, I know what they're like. But I believe in our vision. We have the opportunity to shape a new era for our organization, one that embraces progress and equality."

"Yes, Natasha. We will forge a path that honors our past while embracing the possibilities of the future. The old men may resist, but we will prove them wrong."

I stand and motion for her to sit in front of my laptop. "Back to business."

"Okay. What do you want?"

"I need you to hack into the city's security system and disable the cameras for our target locations."

"Consider it done," she replies, a determined glint in her eye.

"Good," I nod, my voice barely above a whisper.

Natasha's fingers dance gracefully across the keyboard. She is a vision of pure focus, her eyes scanning line after line of code, her sharp mind calculating and analyzing each potential vulnerability in our enemy's defenses. I don't know anything about it, but I'm impressed by the ease with which she handles it.

"Have you found a way in?" I ask.

THE PRICE OF POWER

"Almost," she replies, her fingers never slowing as she continues to search for the perfect opportunity. "Their encryption is good, but not as good as me. You don't have to hover," she says with a slight smirk, finally glancing at me. "I've got this under control."

"Of course, you do," I nod. "But I enjoy watching you work. It's... captivating."

"Flattery will get you everywhere," she teases me, returning her focus to the task at hand. "But for now, let me concentrate."

"Very well," I concede, pushing off from the table and moving toward the bar. As I reach for my favorite whisky, I pause. "Just be careful, Natasha. I have a feeling things are going to get more complicated soon."

"Always am, Kirill," she assured me without looking up. "You know I won't let you down."

"Indeed, I do," I say quietly before I finish my drink.

I allow a smirk to form on my lips; I have no doubt that she will succeed. She always does.

We have both borne the weight of abusive fathers, men who would beat us down physically and mentally. Our shared past has forged a bond between us that nothing could break.

"Got it," Natasha announces triumphantly. "Cameras will be disabled when you give the word."

"Excellent work, as always." I nod. "You know I can't do this without you."

"Of course," she replies, allowing herself a brief smile before returning to her work. "And don't worry, Kirill, I'm not going anywhere. We've come too far together to let anything tear us apart now."

"Indeed," I murmur, my thoughts drifting back to the days when we were nothing more than frightened children. It was a long time ago, but the memories still burn deep within me, reminding me of the pain and suffering we have endured to reach our current positions of power.

"Kirill?" Natasha's voice breaks through my reverie, her expression a mixture of concern and curiosity. "Is everything all right?"

"Of course," I reply, shaking off the momentary lapse in control. "I was just... reminiscing about where we started."

"Ah," she says, understanding flickering in her eyes. "We've come a long way, haven't we?"

"Indeed, we have," I agree. "But there's still so much more to achieve."

"Then let's get to it," Natasha declares, her fingers once again flying across the keyboard.

"Tell me, Natasha," I begin, not bothering to turn around, "do you ever wonder what holds us to this life? To crave control and dominance over others?"

Natasha leans back in my chair, crossing her legs with a casual grace that belies the sharpness of her mind.

"Perhaps it's because we were powerless once," she suggests, her voice carrying a hint of vulnerability. "And we swore never to be so again."

"Powerless... and at the mercy of monsters," I muse, the words tasting sour on my tongue. I finally turn to face Natasha. "No one will ever make us feel that way again."

"Damn right," she agrees fiercely, her eyes blazing with the same fire that fuels her loyalty to me.

"Speaking of which," I say, "I've received word about a certain traitor within our ranks. I want him dealt with - permanently."

"Goran? Are you sure?" Natasha asks, concern lacing her tone as she straightens up. "We could try to extract information from him first, find out what information -"

"Dead men tell no tales, Natasha," I interrupt coldly, cutting her off with a dismissive wave of my hand. "And he certainly can't continue to betray us."

"Very well," she acquiesces, "I'll speak with Vlad, and we'll take care of it."

Vlad is my Enforcer, another person I trust completely.

"Good," I say, "And remember - no loose ends."

"Of course," Natasha replies, her eyes narrowing. She knew better than to question my orders.

As I watch her, I can't help but feel a cold satisfaction settle over me. My past has shaped me into a man who won't stop at anything to protect what is mine, and I won't ever allow anyone to threaten that power or control.

Chapter 2
Emma

The private club pulsates with a symphony of sounds—thumping music, raucous laughter, and the murmur of conversations, creating an atmosphere that is both intoxicating and enticing.

As I lean against the polished mahogany bar, a sense of confidence radiates from within me. My dress, a tantalizing creation of deep red satin, clings to every contour of my body, accentuating my womanly curves with a sinful elegance. The rich crimson serves as a captivating contrast against my porcelain skin. My green eyes framed by long, dark lashes hold a magnetic power. I've known this for a long time. Silken waves of raven hair cascade down my shoulders, caressing my bare skin like the touch of a lover's fingers. My Italian heritage passed down through generations, has gifted me with an irresistible magnetism.

In the beginning, I was intoxicated by the freedom my brothers gave me. It was liberating. I enjoyed it. I longed for it.

I wasn't crossing the lines; everything for the eyes and nothing for the hands, but it was so much more than girls like me could enjoy.

I partied every week. Only here of course, because this club or bar or whatever belongs to our organization. Everybody here belongs to the mafia, to La Morte, and everybody knows who I am. But that didn't dampen my fun. Of course, it's true that

I sometimes colored the stories I told my best friend. Most of it happened in my imagination. And how good those fantasies were.

I'm at the point now where I feel bored, pointless being here.

I want my fantasy.

Want love.

Want to experience raw passion.

Want someone who's not frightened by who my parents, my brothers are. The power they have. Someone who wants me anyway or in spite of it.

I long for the total freedom that I can't find in this setting.

I long to be the one to decide my own destiny.

And I long to finally discover the world of desires.

"Can I get you another drink, Emma?" one of the young bartenders offers, his cheeks flushed from his obvious attraction.

"Sure, why not," I force a flirty smile on myself as I shake off the strange thoughts.

"Emma, there you are!" Gaby calls out, effortlessly weaving through the crowded room. Her brown curls frame her face, and her confident stride makes it clear that she is a woman who knows her place within the organization. As the wife of the Capo of La Morte, Gaby held a position of power and influence, but she never let it come between her friendship with me.

"Emma, it's good to see you finally," Gaby says, enveloping me in a tight embrace. "You look stunning, as always."

Taking a seat next to me, she orders a glass of wine from the bartender before turning her attention to me. "You look like you're enjoying yourself," she teases me, her brown eyes sparkling with mischief.

"Thanks, Gaby. You know me, always trying to make an impression. But appearances can be deceiving," I confide, my voice barely audible over the din of the club. I take a sip of my freshly poured cocktail, the bitter taste momentarily distracting me from my thoughts. "Sometimes... I just... sometimes I wish I could be someone else," I admit, my gaze fixates on the orange liquid swirling in my glass.

"Someone else?" Gaby echoes, concern etches across her face. "What do you mean?"

I hesitate... hesitate to voice my deepest desires. "I'm tired of this. All of this. I don't know my father's plan... This's how I grew up... among them, and so far I've somehow accepted this arranged marriage thing. I didn't like it, but I accepted it as it was, although I hoped my father wasn't so old-fashioned." I'm taking a break to calm down. "He announced that he had started looking for someone for me... But that's not what I want anymore...I want love. True love – the kind that makes your heart race and your soul sing. The kind that can transcend these walls we've built around ourselves... Like yours."

Gaby's expression turns serious as she takes my hand in hers. She squeezes it gently, understanding the sentiment all too well. "That kind of love is rare, Emma. But I believe it exists. And when you find it, it will be worth the wait."

Gaby's loyalty to Luke is unwavering. Despite her own arranged marriage, she has found love within the confines of our world.

But it's rare. I know it.

I nod, my gaze drifting to Victor, Luke's second in command, who stands a few feet away engaged in conversation with some other men. Victor is handsome and charismatic. We have developed a close friendship over the years, sharing secrets and dreams, but I have always wondered if there can be something more between us. I don't know how I feel about this.

"I understand, Gaby," I reply, my voice tinges with a hint of sadness. "But I can't help but hope for a love that's based on more than obligation and duty. I want someone who sees me for who I am, not just as an asset in the world of power and control."

Gaby squeezes my hand. "You deserve nothing less. Love shouldn't be compromised. Keep your heart open, and perhaps the universe will conspire to bring you the love you seek."

"I don't know. Maybe I should rather close my heart so that it doesn't break."

As the conversation unfolded, Luke appeared, his presence commanding the attention of everyone in his path. I watch him. His confident stride and piercing gaze send shivers down my spine. He is the epitome of power and authority, his every word carrying weight within the organization.

Luke approaches Gaby, his eyes full of adoration as he brushes a strand of hair from her face. "My beautiful Gaby," he murmurs, his voice filled with a tenderness that I have rarely witnessed. "You make me proud every day."

Gaby blushes, her voice fills with genuine affection. "And you, Luke, you are my rock. I am forever grateful for your love and protection."

THE PRICE OF POWER

As I observe their exchange, a pang of longing washes over me. I yearn for a connection as deep and genuine as the one shared between them. But I can't ignore the nagging uncertainty that gnaws at my heart.

Victor notices Luke's presence and walks toward us.

"Hi, how are the most beautiful ladies in the world?

We just chuckle at the exaggeration.

Victor takes my hand and pulls me onto the dance floor.

"Emma, what's troubling you?" he asks, his voice gentle yet filled with genuine curiosity.

I force a smile, masking my inner turmoil. "Oh, Vic, it's nothing. Just pondering my place in all of this."

I know that I'm more than just a pretty face, but sometimes it feels like others only see me as a pawn to be used in their games of power and control.

I meet Victor's gaze, and my heart flutters in my chest. I want to confide in him, to share the depths of my longing, but the weight of tradition and fear held me back. I know that Luke's organization is a raditionalist one, where women play secondary roles and men make the decisions.

"Where did this thought come from now?"

"I envy Gaby's love. I want this for myself."

"Really? You're just 19, you'll find love, you have time."

I know he doesn't understand. Men are not that emotional. Or, maybe, they don't really care that much.

"But Vic," I whisper, my voice barely audible above the buzz of the club. "How can I find love in a world where everything is predetermined?"

He shrugs and pulls me closer to him. "What will be will be. But dreams can be dangerous, Emma. They can lead us down paths we're not prepared to walk."

He knows just as well as I do, that I will do what my father says. My parents, long-time members of Luke's organization, are frequently absent, leaving me to be raised by my protective brothers, Seth, Giorgio and Alessio. They have taught me the basics of self-defense and have ingrained in me a sense of loyalty and family above all else.

"Better to have dreams than nothing at all," I counter, unwilling to concede.

After the dance, I'm on my way back to the bar.

"Hey, Emma!" calls out Tony, one of the lower-ranking members of the organization and my former classmate. He is with a group of young people including Lina, who I can't stand.

As I approach them, his eyes scan my body appreciatively. I force a flirtatious smile, batting my eyelashes at him.

"You look stunning today," he says, trying to sound casual but failing miserably.

"Thanks, Tony. What do you need?" I ask, masking my annoyance with practiced ease.

"Will you dance with me?"

"Of course, she will," Lina sneers, her eyes turning sour. "Always gotta be the golden girl, huh? Can't let anyone else shine for a change."

"Jealousy doesn't suit you, Lina," I retort, turning on my heel and striding away before she could respond. I don't give a damn about them.

"Emma, have you met Marco?" Gaby asks as I sit next to her at the bar, nodding toward a man who is speaking with Luca.

He is tall, with dark hair and piercing blue eyes that seem to see right through me. His confident stride commands attention, and I can't help but feel a little intimidated by his presence.

"No, I haven't," I reply, trying to sound nonchalant while my heart pounds in my chest. I have heard whispers about Marco – a new member of the organization who has quickly risen through the ranks due to his strategic prowess and uncanny ability to get information.

"Marco, this is Emma," Gaby introduces us, and I extend my hand, forcing a smile onto my face as we shake hands. His grip is firm, yet gentle, sending an unexpected shiver down my spine.

"Nice to meet you, Emma," Marco says, his voice carrying a hint of an accent that I can't quite place. "I've heard a lot about you and your beauty."

"Thank you," I reply, feeling my cheeks flush at the compliment.

A silence follows, filled only with the sounds of music and murmured conversations from others in the club. My thoughts race – what does he really know about me? What does he think of me? And why do I care so much about the opinions of a man I have just met?

"Maybe we can dance?" Marco suggests.

"Sure," I agree, although the thought of dancing with him made my stomach churn with a mix of excitement and dread. Is it possible that I'm actually attracted to someone within the organization?

I look at Luke, but I can't read anything in his eyes. I enjoy relative freedom, thanks to my brothers, but there is a line I can't cross.

I know the limits. What I can and cannot do.

My brothers aren't here now but they know that Gaby, and more importantly Luke and Victor, will be here.

Since Luke has no objection to dancing, I go to the dancefloor, Marco close behind me.

The next day, at home I can't help but ponder the possibility of a relationship with someone like Marco. He is attractive and intelligent, yet also undeniably dangerous. Can I ever truly trust someone who is in this life, or will they simply use me for their own gain?

I reach for my phone and lie down on my bed while I ring Gaby.

"Hey, Emma. Everything okay?" she asks.

"Of course," I lie. "I'm just... thinking."

"About that new guy, Marco?" Gaby asks. "He certainly seems smitten."

"Maybe," I admit hesitantly, my cheeks warming at the thought. "But you know how it is here. Relationships can be... complicated."

"True," Gaby concedes, sobering a bit. "But sometimes, they're worth fighting for. Just remember - you don't have to do this alone. I'll always be here for you, no matter what."

"Thanks, Gaby," I whisper.

"Besides," Gaby adds with a mischievous hint in her voice, "if anyone can handle the twists and turns of mafia life, it's you."

I can't help but laugh, grateful for the momentary reprieve from my worries. "And if I ever need backup, I know who to call."

"Damn right," Gaby agrees, laughing along with me.

"Whatever the future holds," I whisper to myself, "I won't face it alone."

After I hung up, I see myself in the mirror and make a silent vow to myself. I will not settle for anything less than a love that would light up my world, a love that will defy the darkness surrounding us.

Chapter 3
Kirill

The air in Luke's private office hangs heavy with tension as Luke and I face each other across the oak desk. The room, adorned with opulent furnishings, bears witness to the wealth and influence that Luke commands within the criminal underworld. Our eyes lock in a battle of dominance and control.

"Let's get to the point," I say in a low, steady voice, my eyes never leaving the faces of the men present. "I have made my decision regarding the woman I am to marry. It's time to unite not only in business but also in blood."

The room falls into an expectant silence as the significance of my words settles upon them.

Will this union truly bring peace between us, or will it only serve to fan the flames of our long-standing feud? I pray silently that it is the former, that this bond forged in blood will be the catalyst for a new era of cooperation and prosperity.

As I lean back in my chair, the supple leather creaks under my weight. My eyes lock on Luke. His fingers tap rhythmically on the polished surface of the table, a subtle display of his impatience.

"Emma Gallo," I announce. The name rolls off my tongue like a sacred word. "She will be my wife."

Luke's brow furrows with surprise. He reclines in his chair, his posture relaxed but his gaze sharp and penetrating. "You

27

want to marry Emma? She's Gaby's best friend, Kirill. This can complicate things."

Natasha straightens beside me. The name wasn't unexpected, we had already discussed everything. She wasn't very happy about it, but she accepted my choice.

Opposite Natasha sits Victor, Luke's loyal and fiercely protective second in command. He shows a stoic expression, his arms cross over his chest, his steely eyes fix on the interplay between us. His body exudes an aura of readiness, prepared to defend his boss at a moment's notice.

Outside the windows, the sound of rain tapping against the glass provides a haunting backdrop. Lightning occasionally illuminates the room, casting fleeting flashes of stark brightness.

My gaze never wavers. "Da," I reply my voice colder than ice. I know the risks, but I also know the potential rewards. "I understand your concerns, but I've thought this through. Emma is the woman I want by my side. She possesses qualities that I find captivating, and I believe this union will strengthen our alliance."

Luke's gaze hardens as he stares at me.

He sighs, running a hand through his black hair. "You're playing with fire. Gaby won't be pleased with this turn of events. I know how fiercely she guards her friendships." Luke looks at Victor for a moment.

"I understand Gaby's loyalty, Luke, but this is a decision I can't and won't compromise on."

My heart skips a beat, but for now, I keep this fire that threatens to burn me, hidden deep within me, as I have been taught since childhood. After all, there is much to be done before we can truly call ourselves allies – and even more, before I can claim Emma as my own.

Luke studies me for a moment, his piercing gaze attempting to unravel me.

I lean forward, my voice low and measured. "Luke, I understand the risks involved in this alliance. But together, our organizations will become a force that can't be reckoned with."

Luke is still deep in thought. I understand his doubts, but I'm not going to let this go. Let her go.

"Luke, we have no intention of betraying this alliance. Our focus is on expanding our reach, not internal power struggles." Natasha's voice is cool and confident.

Victor leans forward, his tone skeptical. "Kirill, can we trust you to keep your word? This marriage is more than just an arrangement – it's a merging of our lives and operations. The consequences of betrayal are severe."

I lock eyes with him. "Victor, I give you my word as the leader of Diabol. My commitment to this alliance is unwavering. But know that any betrayal will not go unanswered."

"Likewise, Kirill. Our families have a long history. Let it be known that breaking this bond will have dire consequences," Luke nods.

The room falls into a heavy silence.

"Luke, let's not underestimate the power of this unity. We may not trust each other completely, but our common goals outweigh our doubts. We can both benefit from this alliance," I say.

Luke smirks."True, Kirill. It seems we find ourselves in a peculiar situation. Who would have thought that our rivalry would lead to such an unexpected turn of events?"

"Then, Emma?" I ask because we are completely off the original point.

"Very well," Luke finally concedes, resignation settling in his voice. "If this is truly what you want, let be."

"Thank you, Luke."

A sense of triumph washes over me, mingled with a touch of satisfaction. My heart hammers in my chest. The fire that burns within me, fueled by a long-held obsession, dances with anticipation at the prospect of this union. It is more than mere strategy; it is a hunger, an insatiable craving to conquer both the underworld and the heart of the woman who will bear my name. I have kept my feelings for Emma hidden, safeguarding them like a prized possession. Emma, the woman I have secretly admired from afar, will be mine. The thought sends a surge of anticipation through my veins.

But amidst the elation, there is also a hint of caution. I know that this alliance, built on the fragile foundation of deception, carries its own risks. It is a delicate dance, a game of calculated moves and hidden motives. I can't afford to let my guard down, even as my heart flutters with the possibility of a connection that goes beyond the realm of power and control.

As I leave Luke's office, my mind swirls with conflicting emotions. I have always prided myself on being cold and ruthless, unyielding in my pursuit of power. But Emma holds the possibility to shatter my carefully constructed facade.

My lips curl into a smile as I envision the future. I see myself by Emma's side, our union symbolizing strength and dominance. I imagine the fire between us, a passion that burns brighter than the city lights outside my window. It is a desire that consumes me, a hunger that refuses to be sated.

But for now, I must bide my time, keep my emotions in check. The game is far from over, and I must tread carefully, navigating the treacherous path that lies ahead.

I revel in the knowledge that my plan is in motion, that destiny has brought me closer to the woman who has captured my attention.

I drive straight to my office, and can't stand it any longer, I turn on my laptop. *What are you doing, moja dorogaja?* My eyes glue to the laptop screen. It is a live feed of Emma in her bedroom, the soft light from her bedside lamp illuminating her delicate features. My breath catches as she brushes a stray lock of hair behind her ear, her fingers lingering on her neck for just a moment.

Natasha has hacked her laptop so I can follow her every move via the webcam.

Her every conversation.

Her every night.

"God, she's exquisite," I murmur. The desire to possess her consumes me.

I crave the power to control her every movement and dictate her every emotion. I know it's twisted, but I can't help myself.

Emma has become an obsession, and the dark satisfaction I feel from watching her is overpowering.

"Enjoying the view?" Natasha's sultry voice cut through my thoughts like a knife, causing me to jump. Damn her impeccable timing but I don't take my eyes off the monitor.

"Natasha, what do you want?" I snap, not bothering to hide the irritation in my voice.

"Relax, boss" she teases, leaning against the doorframe with a grin. "I just came to tell you that we're finished with the project."

I'm not really paying attention, so I don't know what she's talking about at first. Then it pops in and I pick my head up. "Marco?"

The little bastard. He touched her. Held her in his arms while they danced. I can't stand it. Emma is mine. All he had to do was keep an eye on her. Nothing more. Even though he belonged to Luke's organization, even that couldn't save him. I didn't care about anything, not even the alliance. No one could touch her. No one but me.

Natasha nods.

"Perfect. Now leave me alone, I have work to do."

But Natasha wasn't one to be easily dismissed.

"Really? Because from where I'm standing, it looks like you're more interested in watching her than working," Natasha taunts, crossing her arms over her chest.

"Your opinion was not requested," I say. "Now, go."

"Yeah, I see" Natasha sighs theatrically, pushing away from the doorframe. "But don't forget Kirill, we have other things to do too."

"Your concern is touching, but unnecessary" I retort, my eyes never leaving the screen. "I know what I'm doing."

"Good," and she turns to leave. "But just remember, I'm always here if you need me." And with that, she disappears down the hallway.

THE PRICE OF POWER

I turn back to the screen, my heart racing as some strange sensation courses through my veins. I know Natasha is right; my obsession with Emma is dangerous. But I can't help it. She is like a drug, and I am addicted.

"Damn you, Emma" I mutter under my breath, my gaze fixed on her sleeping form. "Why do you have to be so... perfect?"

"Oooh" she moans in her sleep, her voice like a siren's call. My heart clenches at the sound, and I feel my cock begin to stir in my pants.

"Shhh" I whisper, imagining what it will be like to hold her in my arms, to feel her soft skin beneath my fingertips. The thought sends a shiver down my spine and my dick is painfully hard. I could take it out and jerk it off, but I don't do it.

"Soon" I growl, slamming my laptop shut.

I need to speed things up. Emma will finally be mine, and no one can stop me.

"Get ready, my dear" I whisper into the shadows. "Your world is about to change forever."

Chapter 4
Emma

My father sits on the couch next to the table, his hands clasped tightly together. My brothers flank our father, their jaws clenched.

What's going on?

Luke stands at the center of the study, accompanied by Victor.

My heart races as I take my seat in the middle of the room.

Luke clears his throat, breaking the silence. "Emma, you know how important the alliance with the Diabol is to our family, don't you?" he asks gently, placing a comforting hand on my shoulder.

I nod, swallowing hard. "I do, Luke."

Actually, I don't know. I have no idea why Luke starts talking business with me. Women don't get involved in this kind of thing. I glance at my father, but he avoids my eyes. Seth presses his lips into a thin line, and Alessio furrows his eyebrows. *What's going on?*

Luke arrived with Victor and retreated with the male members of my family to my father's study. Now I've been asked to join them.

"Arranged marriages are common among our kind," he continues, his voice low and soothing. "I married your best friend that way, and I can't imagine my life without her," he pauses, searching my eyes. "Kirill has proposed to marry you, Emma."

Everything stops.

I can't breathe.

I can't hear... I can't feel anything.

My heart is pounding in my ears.

My vision blurs.

I don't believe it. I can't believe it.

I look pleadingly at my father. His gaze drifts to the polished surface of the table, unable to meet my eyes. "Emma, my dear, sometimes sacrifices must be made for the greater good. We have a responsibility to the family, to protect and secure our future. This marriage is an opportunity to strengthen our position."

Alessio slams his fist on the table, his voice laced with anger. "Father, how can you expect Emma to marry a man rumored to be as ruthless as Kirill? We've heard the stories, the whispers of his cruelty. How can we do this to her?"

Luke's gaze hardens, his voice firm. "Alessio, I understand your concerns but I won't tolerate that tone. Don't forget who I am. I know this is a family matter, but your father and I made an agreement. Kirill is a man of power and influence, and he has proven himself capable of protecting those he holds dear."

"You speak of safety and stability, but what about love? What about Emma's happiness? How can you ask her to sacrifice that?"

Victor steps forward, his tone measured. "Alessio, we must remember that love doesn't always come in the form of grand romances. Sometimes it grows slowly, over time, nurtured by respect and trust. Kirill may not be known for his tenderness, but he is a man of honor. Emma, with time, you may find a connection, a partnership that will provide you with the support and protection you deserve."

My heart sinks, torn between duty and my own desires. How can I possibly marry a man I don't know? A man whose ruthlessness is whispered about in hushed tones?

"Is this truly what's best for us?" I look to Luke, my voice barely above a whisper.

Luke's expression softens, a flicker of sympathy crossing his eyes. "It's not ideal, but it's necessary."

As I gaze around the room, I know I can't let them down. I'll do this for them, even if it means sacrificing my own chance at true love.

My eyes well up with tears. "All right," I whisper. "I'll marry him."

At my acceptance, the room buzzed with a mix of relief and unease. I exchange wary glances with my brothers. At least they tried. Not many people dare to defy the Capo.

I stay in front of my bathroom mirror, staring at my reflection as I try to process what has just happened. I can't believe that I have agreed to marry Kirill, a man I don't know, all for the sake of our alliance with his powerful Russian mafia. My eyes widen, and my mouth hangs slightly open in shock. *Shit! What have I done?*

"Is this really happening?" I whisper to myself, my heart pounding in my chest as if I have run. The thought of marrying someone I don't love terrifies me, but this damn loyalty to my family I've been raised with is too strong to ignore.

My phone rings.

"Emma, are you all right? I've just heard," Gaby's concerned voice echos through the line.

"Uh, yeah," I reply, trying to steady my voice. I'm still in shock. "I'm fine. Just... processing everything."

"I am so mad at Luke for putting you in this position."

"Don't be. Kirill or someone else? It makes no difference." *There is a difference*, whispers a small voice in my head.

"Are you okay with it then?"

Okay? No! I'm afraid. I'm afraid of what marrying Kirill means to me.

She knows me too well. I sigh. I didn't want to upset her or put a wedge between her and Luke, but I have to be honest with someone. "I've heard rumors about the things he's done in the past. How can I trust him?"

"Emma, we all have our pasts, but what truly matters is the present and the future we choose to build.

"But Gaby, what if I'm making a mistake? What if I can't love him? Can't stand him?"

"Emma, no relationship is without its challenges. Love has the power to heal and transform, to bring out the best in us. Have faith in yourself."

I stay in front of the full-length mirror, my gaze fixed on the reflection that stares back at me. The room is suffused with the glow of the afternoon light, filtering through the curtains and casting a gentle haze over the space. The air holds the scent of fresh flowers. My fingertips brush against the delicate white lace of my wedding gown, tracing the intricate patterns that adorn the fabric. As my hands smooth down the dress, a shiver of anxiety courses through me, causing my heart to quicken its pace. I hear the distant murmur of voices outside, the excited whispers of the wedding guests, mingling with the subtle melodies of classical music that flow through the air.

This day has come too soon. Only a month has passed since the meeting. Meeting? I wouldn't call it that.

I straighten my veil, its weight in my hair reminds me of my responsibilities, the gravity of the decision I have made.

As the minutes tick away, my unease grows, casting a shadow over the beauty of the moment.

The weight of my decision settles upon me like a heavy cloak, causing me to question the path I have chosen.

There is nothing more to be done. I steel myself, summoning the strength to face the unknown.

"Alright," I say out loud. "I can do this."

As the wedding march begins to play, and I walk down the aisle on my father's arm, my gaze searches Kirill. He stands tall and imposing, his black hair perfectly styled and a hint of stubble gracing his chiseled jawline. His piercing ice-blue eyes captivate me but his expression is stoic, almost unreadable. His gaze softens as he beheld me in my bridal glory. I feel the weight of his intense gaze, a mixture of curiosity and calculation that sends a shiver down my spine. My footsteps falter momentarily, but I gather my courage and continue my march toward him.

Kirill's presence is magnetic, commanding the attention of everyone in the room. Dressed in a tailored black suit, he exudes an air of authority and power. His chiseled features are softened by the flickering candlelight, and as I approach, I can't help but notice the slight curl of his lips.

The priest's voice fills the air, his words a solemn reminder of the sacred union about to take place. My gaze locks with Kirill's as we exchange the vows. My heart races as his hand gently cuppes my cheek, drawing me closer. Our lips meet in a hesitant, yet electric, kiss.

I close my eyes.

The taste of him is intoxicating, a blend of mint and warmth that lingers on my lips. I feel the subtle stubble of his jaw against my skin, a reminder of his masculinity.

The touch is soft, tender, yet there is an underlying intensity that makes my pulse quicken. Our mouths move in a slow, exploratory dance. My fingers instinctively curl into the fabric of Kirill's suit, seeking an anchor in the sea of sensations.

I savor the moment, the mingling of our breaths, and the subtle sighs that escape between our lips.

After the ceremony, the celebration moves to the Merkur Hotel's hall adorned with opulent decorations. The room is filled with the soft glow of candlelight, casting a romantic ambiance over the gathering. I take my place at the head table, my heart fluttering as I steal glances at Kirill, who sits beside me.

The clinking of glasses signals the beginning of the dinner, and conversations fill the room.

Kirill leans towards me, his voice low and captivating. "You look exquisite tonight, Emma," he murmurs, his gaze tracing the delicate curve of my neck.

His icy blue eyes meet mine causing an involuntary shiver to run down my spine.

"I... I appreciate your kind words, Kirill, but I must admit, I'm still trying to understand all of this."

THE PRICE OF POWER

A flicker of understanding passes through his eyes, his expression softening. "I understand your apprehension, Emma," he admits, his voice tinges with a hint of regret. "Our circumstances may be unconventional, but I promise you, I will do my utmost to ensure your happiness and safety."

My heart flutters at his words, a glimmer of hope blossoming within me.

I have expected cold indifference or even hostility from him, but his genuine concern touches something deep within me.

"Shall we dance?" he grants me with a smile that sends my heart into overdrive.

He stands up and offers his hand, his eyes never leaving mine. My trembling hand finds its place in his firm grasp. I can feel the heat of his palm against my skin, a jolt of electricity coursing through me. The room seems to fade away.

Our bodies move in a harmonious rhythm, our steps perfectly in sync. My heart races as I catch the scent of Kirill's cologne, a subtle blend of musk and spice. With each twirl and dip, I feel Kirill's firm yet gentle grip, guiding me with confidence and precision. His touch sent shivers down my spine, awakening a desire that I have never felt before. It's a dance of seduction, a silent conversation in the language of touch and movement. Our eyes lock, and I am captivated by its intensity.

There is a hunger there.

It is a magnetic pull, drawing us closer.

Kirill's hand slides sensually down my back, pulling me even closer. The heat of his body radiates through the thin fabric. My breath hitches. The room around us seems to fade into a blur as we move as one.

The final notes of the music echo through the room, and I find myself breathless, my hand still lingering in Kirill's warm grasp, and as the applause erupts around us, I can't help but wonder what lay ahead of us.

Chapter 5

Kirill

The thick oak door creaks open as I lead Emma into my penthouse apartment. Anticipation swirls in my stomach. Finally.

This is our wedding night.

Emma takes in a sharp breath as my hand finds the bare skin of her back.

"There's no need to be nervous, malyshka," I purr against her ear. My voice is like velvet, soft and soothing. Yet there is an edge to it, I can't hide. "I'm going to take good care of you tonight. We'll take it slow, I promise."

She swallows hard and nods.

I see her hesitation and pause in the foyer, turning to face her.

"You have my word, Emma. I will never hurt you." My hand slides up to cup her cheek and she leans into my touch. "Tonight, and every night after, I'm going to show you pleasure like you've never known."

A blush stains her cheeks at my bold promise.

I know she is afraid, but there's no reason to be. We have to consummate this marriage and she knows it. It's the only way to make this alliance complete.

But the alliance is the last thing on my mind.

I can't keep my hands off her any longer.

I can't hold back this desire any longer.

I must have her.

She is still a virgin, I warn myself. *And you're 28, not a horny teenager*.

Her virginity is a bonus. I know all about her. Everything there is to know. Ever since I saw her in that sexy dress she wore to Luke's private club, I've had my eyes on her. I know the role she plays for the outside world. I even bugged her phone.

I'm not ashamed. I have all the tools, so why not use them? I've done far worse things. And this is not bad.

She's a miracle.

A treasure.

And she's mine. Only mine.

Her breaths quicken as I dip my head to capture her mouth in a searing kiss. My tongue circles lazily in her mouth. It ignites a slow, delicious burn deep in my belly.

By the time I break the kiss, Emma is panting. She stares up at me with half-lidded eyes. I see desire sparkling in them.

She wants me—wants this.

Something in me snaps at the sight.

I can't wait any longer. My self-control is dancing on the brink.

I take her hand and lead her into my bedroom. Candles flicker on every surface, bathing the room in a warm, sensual glow.

Emma's gaze darts to the large bed in the center of the room, its black silk sheets an open invitation, and her eyes widen. Her whole body tenses again. I come up behind her, my hands settling on her hips.

"Relax, malyshka," I murmur against her neck. "I won't hurt you."

She nods, a soft whimper escaping her as my lips brush over the sensitive skin below her ear. So responsive. She may be afraid of all this, but her body responds to my touch.

Good. Very good. I can work with that.

My hand slides around to the front of her dress and rests on the tempting bumps. My other hand slowly pulls the zipper down her back. I let the silky fabric slip down Emma's body to pool at her feet, leaving her in only her lace bra and panties.

I turn her to face me, my gaze raking hungrily over her near-naked form. "So beautiful," I purr, cupping her breasts through the delicate lace. "I've waited so long for this moment."

It is completely different to see her naked in my bedroom than on the screen.

So much better.

So much more beautiful.

It's as if a veil has been lifted, revealing her true beauty in a way that no screen could ever capture. Every curve, every contour of her body is now laid bare before my eyes, and I can't help but be captivated by her exquisite form. Her curves are a work of art, a masterpiece that I have the privilege of beholding.

Heat floods her cheeks at the evidence of my desire straining against the front of my slacks. I notice her gaze and smile, slowly unbuckling my belt. She bites her lips but doesn't look away as I push my pants and boxers down, freeing my erection. I stroke it.

Emma swallows hard.

I tilt her chin up, forcing her to meet my eyes. "Don't be afraid, Emma. I'll go slow." My thumb brushes over her lower lip. "Just relax and enjoy."

Emma nods with wide eyes. I guide her onto the bed and follow her down, bracing myself above her on my forearms as I claim her mouth in a searing kiss.

She moans into my mouth. My hands roam over her body, squeezing her breasts and hips. My head follows my hands taking one lace-covered nipple into my mouth, swirling my tongue around it and eliciting a soft moan from Emma. Her fingers tangle in my hair, urging me on.

Yes. She wants this as much as me.

I slip my hand under the thin lace of her panties. Emma gasps as my fingers find her wet heat, circling and teasing.

I raise my head, gazing down at her. "So responsive," I purr, nipping at her jaw now. "I can't wait to be inside you."

She squirms under my touch, soft cries escaping her lips.

"Shh, easy now," I soothe. I slide down her body, trailing kisses over her collarbone and breasts. Emma whimpers as I free one nipple from her bra, drawing the sensitive bud into my mouth.

She strokes my arms, back.

"Please," she gasps.

I release her nipple with a wet pop, gazing up at her through my hooded eyes. "What is it you want, Emma?" My fingers stroke teasingly over her entrance. "Tell me."

"You," she breathes. "I want you inside me."

A smile curves my lips. "As you wish."

I sit back on my heels and strip off my shirt and boxers before returning to her. Emma sits up, unhooks her bra and throws it on the floor. I hook my fingers under the waistband of her panties. In one smooth motion, I strip them off, baring her completely to my gaze. And my God, this is a sight to behold.

I can't get enough of it. Emma squeezes her eyes shut, heat flooding her cheeks.

"Look at me, Emma."

She opens her eyes. "You're exquisite. And now, you're mine."

I lean down and captured Emma's lips in a searing kiss as I settle between her thighs. Emma moans into my mouth, her hands roaming over my back and shoulders.

When I break the kiss, I rasp, "This may hurt at first, but I will be gentle. You must relax for me, Emma."

She nods.

I reach down between us, guiding myself to her entrance. Emma tenses as she feels the broad head of my cock nudges against her, then with a sigh she forces herself to relax.

"Good girl," I murmur.

I push into her slowly, inch by inch, stopping when she grimaces and tenses. "Breathe, Emma."

I'm watching intently until she does.

I give another shallow thrust, then another, until I am seated fully.

"You're so tight," I groan. "So perfect, moya koroleva."

I remain still, giving her time to adjust. When she rocks her hips experimentally, I am rewarded with a spike of pleasure.

"Move," she pleads. "Please, Kirill."

"As you wish.". I draw back slowly before surging forward again. Emma cries out.

Yes, this is what she has craved. What we have both craved.

I set a steady rhythm, my strokes deep and powerful. With each thrust, I pour my devotion into her, letting her know that she is cherished, desired, and adored. Emma meets each thrust eagerly, clinging to me until she shatters, flinging her into an abyss of bliss.

I groan her name, my movements turning erratic. Something snaps inside me and I can't restrain myself anymore. I know I'm more intense with her than I had planned. More as her first time requires. But I can't stop myself. I've waited too long for this. As I find my own release, I collapse against her, my heart pounding as wildly as hers.

I press a tender kiss on her forehead. "You were exquisite, malyshka. I'm the luckiest man alive to have you as my wife."

" It was amazing. And I'm lucky to have you," she said softly.

"You'll always be safe with me," I promise. "I won't let anyone hurt you. Not ever." I know the risks that come with being the wife of a mafia boss. There are enemies who won't hesitate to strike.

Emma swallows.

"I know," she says. "I feel safe with you."

She smiles and initiates a kiss, and desire stir anew inside me but I suppress it. It was the first time for her, she must still be sore. My cock is hard again so I push my hips back a little so she doesn't feel it. She curls up at my side and draws various zigzag patterns on my chest. I'm glad she took the consummation of our marriage so easily.

"Can I ask you a question?"

"Sure. Anything."

"Who was the woman who sat next to you at the reception?"

She doesn't look me in the eye, just watches her fingers, but as the rhythm of her breathing changes, I know she cares about the answer.

"Natasha?"

She just shrugs. I know she's thinking of her.

I hesitate, struggling to find the right way to begin.

"She is my Consigliere."

She throws her head up in disbelief. "She?"

I prop myself up on my elbow to meet her gaze. This is important. "Indeed, she is."

"But...but she is a woman, " she whispers.

"Yes," I chuckle. "But I trust her. She's been by my side since we were children, and her loyalty to me and the organization is unmatched. She possesses a brilliant mind and exceptional skills in the digital realm."

Emma's brow furrows inquisitively. "The digital realm? What do you mean?"

I smirk, my fingers gently tracing patterns on her bare arm. Gooseskin appears in its wake, and it is satisfying to watch. "I believe in adapting to the changing times, Emma. The web offers boundless possibilities for expanding our influence and operations. With Natasha's expertise, we can tap into the digital world and create a new kind of power."

She nods, absorbing my words. "But doesn't that come with risks? The online world is vast and unpredictable."

"Indeed, there are risks. But with risk comes reward, Emma. We have the opportunity to reach new territories, establish connections, and stay steps ahead of our adversaries. Natasha's involvement will ensure our seamless integration into this digital landscape."

Emma's gaze deepens, and her fingers stop mine. "And what about your history, Kirill? The rumors I've heard about you and your ruthlessness?"

My thumb traces gentle circles on the back of her hand. "Those rumors are just that, Emma. Rumors. I won't deny that my past is checkered, but it's precisely that past that has led me to where I am today. I've learned from my experiences and grown stronger. As for you, I want you to know that you are safe with me."

Emma's eyes search mine, a mixture of uncertainty and curiosity. "Safe? Can anyone truly be safe in this world?"

"I won't make false promises, Emma. But I can promise you this: I will do everything in my power to protect you. You're not just a pawn in a game."

"I want to learn everything about you – the good, the bad, and everything in between."

"We have a lifetime," I say as she yawns.

"I want to know more about you – the man behind the mafia boss."

I look at her surprised. "What do you want to know?"

"Tell me about your dreams, your passions... What truly makes you happy?"

I have to think hard. "My mother loved to paint. I have heard, she often was lost in her own world of colors and brushstrokes. I suppose I inherited that love for art from her."

"Really?" Emma's eyes sparkled with intrigue. "Have you ever painted something yourself?"

"Once," I admit. "But it's been a long time since I've picked up a brush."

"Maybe we could try painting together someday," Emma suggests, her voice filled with excitement and hope.

"I'd like that," I reply with a smile. "Your turn," I prompt, gently stroking her cheek. "What are some things people don't know about you?"

Emma took a deep breath, considering her response. "Well, I've always loved dancing but it's not a secret. I love it."

"Then we should dance together," I say.

"Thank you," she whispers slowly. Her eyes are already closed and after a few moments, her chest moves at a steady pace.

"Good night, dorogaya" I whisper and kiss her forehead.

Chapter 6

Emma

The dim lighting of the Russian mafia-owned restaurant reflects off the polished glassware, casting a gentle glow on the intimate booth where we sit.

I fiddle with the silverware while we wait for our appetizer to arrive.

"Emma," Kirill purrs, as he reaches across the table to stop my hand. His touch sends shivers down my spine, awakening a deep desire within me. "You look absolutely stunning tonight."

"Thank you," I reply, averting my gaze momentarily. I still couldn't get used to the feeling what a single touch of his hand can give me. I had no idea I was so passionate. It was as if Kirill had opened a door in me. I'm insatiable. Unsatisfiable. One touch from him and I'm on fire.

It is only a few weeks after our wedding. I can't say Kirill doesn't try. He reads my wishes by day. And at night... at night, everything is covered in passion. I didn't think such a thing could exist. He plays with my body like a master or rather a devil.

"Tell me something, moya zhena," Kirill continues, using the Russian term of endearment that makes me feel both cherished and owned. It means my wife. That much I have already learned. "Do you enjoy these little outings of ours?" His cold blue eyes bore into mine, searching for any hint of insincerity.

"I do," I admit, my voice barely above a whisper. "Nice of you to bring me on a date so we can get to know each other better."

I really do. He doesn't have to do it, and I appreciate that. Even if in a normal relationship these things are reversed.

"Good," Kirill murmurs, satisfied.

I shift in my seat, the slit in my black dress riding up my thigh. My pulse quickens as Kirill's gaze follows the movement and a predatory gleam appears in his icy eyes. He leans closer, his lips brushing against my ear as he whispers salacious promises that send heat coursing through my veins. I can't deny the powerful attraction between us.

"Kirill," I breathe, my resistance crumbling beneath his seductive advances. "I want you too... but...not here." The thought of exposing myself, regardless of the erotic thrill it provided, causes me to stop this. Him.

"Indeed, my love. You're right, " he teases, his fingers tracing idle patterns on the exposed skin of my thigh. "The night is still young, and we have plenty of time to explore each other's desires."

As we speak, I can't help but notice the way the other patrons defer to Kirill, their eyes filled with a mix of respect and fear. It is clear that my husband's reputation preceded him, and I find myself both attracted and repelled by the ruthless power he wielded.

The restaurant's romantic atmosphere is momentarily disrupted when a large man with gray hair and cold eyes enters the room. I recognize him as Jurij, Kirill's father's former Consigliere. I have heard whispers of his ruthless nature and cunning mind, but this is the first time I've met the man in person. Natasha follows closely behind him, her mouth pursed in anger.

"Ah, Kirill," Jurij says, approaching our table with a broad smile. "It's so good to see you again. And this must be your lovely bride, Emma."

"Jurij," Kirill replies, his voice tight with barely concealed disdain. "What brings you here?"

"Can't an old friend come to congratulate the happy couple?" he asks, taking a seat without being invited.

I feel a pang of jealousy as Natasha appears at our table, her presence a stark contrast to Jurij's menacing aura. I can't help but admire the young woman's confidence and poise.

"Natasha," Jurij sneers, casting her a dismissive glance. "Still playing second fiddle to our dear Kirill, I see."

"Unlike some people, I know my place," Natasha retorts, her voice icy. "I told you not to bother Kirill now."

"Your insolence is unbecoming," Jurij spits, turning his attention to me. "Tell me, Mrs. Volkov, do you truly believe you're worthy of standing by Kirill's side?"

My cheeks flush, but before I can respond, Kirill grabs Jurij's wrist in a vice-like grip, his face a mask of fury. "Don't you dare speak to my wife like that," he snarls.

"Kirill, please," I place a hand on his arm in an attempt to calm him. But it is too late. With a swift, brutal motion, Kirill twists Jurij's wrist, snapping the bones with a sickening crunch. Jurij screams in pain.

"Let that be a lesson to you," Kirill says coldly, releasing Jurij's mangled wrist. "I will not tolerate disrespect."

As Jurij is dragged away by two burly men, I shudder at the violence I've just witnessed – and the unsettling thrill it sent through my body. I feel Natasha touch my shoulder gently, offering a compassionate smile.

"Are you alright?" she asks, genuine concern in her eyes.

"Y-yes," I stammer, still reeling from the scene. "Thank you."

"I hope no one else will interrupt our evening." Kirill looks at Natasha with a pointed look.

"I'm sure not. Enjoy your dinner."

I look after Natasha for a long time. I like the cool confidence that surrounds her.

"Would you like to dance?" Kirill offers his hand.

"Of course," I agree, my heart flutters in anticipation.

We dance on all our dates. I love to snuggle up to him, feel his warm body against mine and sway softly to the music, forgetting the world around us.

However, I can't relax now. Our bodies are pressed tightly against each other, and I feel a thrill of excitement mixed with fear. I'm aware of the danger that lurks beneath the surface of this world – the constant threat of betrayal, violence, and death.

"Are you afraid?" Kirill whispers into my ear as he pulls me even closer, his breath hot against my skin.

"Should I be?" I ask, trying to maintain my composure despite the trepidation that tightens my chest.

"Only if you let it control you," he murmurs, nipping playfully at my earlobe before releasing me from his embrace. "We are all masters of our own destiny, my love. Remember that."

I step closer, stand on tiptoe and kiss him. My concerns fade as desire ignites in my blood. The kiss turns possessive and all-consuming. He is staking his claim on me in a way that makes me feel cherished and possessed all at once.

When he finally releases my lips, I'm breathless.

"Take me home," I whisper. I need to lose myself in his touch and forget about the darkness that lingers at the edges of my new life.

Kirill's eyes gleam with lust and something more primal. "It will be my pleasure." He throws some bills on the table and ushers me out of the restaurant.

In the back of his car, Kirill wastes no time pinning me against the leather seat and ravishing my neck with hot, open-mouthed kisses. I gasp, threading my fingers through his hair and holding him close. I spread my legs, aching for the hardness I can feel straining against his trousers.

"Emma," Kirill whispers, his voice low and seductive. His ice-blue eyes lock onto mine, filled with a hunger I can't help but respond to. "You have no idea how much I've wanted this."

A shiver runs down my spine as I feel his hand slowly slide up my thigh. My heart races in my chest, and I bite my lip, trying to suppress a moan. I can't resist him. Something about Kirill draws me in, even though I know I should be stronger. It's just physical attraction. Nothing more, I soothe myself.

"Tell me you want this too," he demands, the intensity of his gaze never wavering.

His words ignite a fire within me that I can't control. "Yes," I breathe out, my voice barely audible. "I want it, Kirill."

"Good." He smirks, knowing he has me under his spell. "Because I plan on making you scream my name tonight."

My core pulses with need as he leans in closer to me, his lips brushing against mine. As he deepens the kiss, his hands roam over my body, pulling at my clothes with a frenzied urgency.

"God, Emma, you're driving me insane," he mutters against my skin as he pushes my dress higher, revealing my black lace panties. "You're so fucking perfect."

In this moment, I don't care where we are, that anyone can see us; all I want is Kirill.

He hooks one finger around the delicate fabric of my underwear, yanking it aside before plunging two fingers into me. I gasp, my back arching off the seat as sensation overwhelms me.

"Kirill!" I cry out, unable to keep quiet any longer. He smirks at my reaction, his fingers working their magic inside of me while his other hand pinches and teases one of my nipples through the thin fabric of my bra.

"Such a beautiful sound," he murmurs, his eyes dark with lust. "But I want more."

He withdraws his fingers abruptly, leaving me feeling empty and desperate for more. Before I can protest, he unzips his pants and positions himself between my legs. My body trembles with excitement as he lines up his thick length, teasing my entrance with the head of his cock.

"Ready?" he asks, his voice rough with desire.

"Please," I beg, my need for him consuming all rational thought.

With a wicked grin, he pushes into me, filling me completely. I cry out in a mixture of pain and pleasure, my nails digging into his shoulders. I crave this intimacy and raw passion that Kirill provides.

"Fuck, Emma," he grunts, his hips slamming against mine, each thrust more powerful than the last. "You feel so good around me."

"Kirill, don't stop," I plead, my orgasm building rapidly as he pounds into me without mercy. He obliges, thrusting into me harder and faster, driving us both toward the edge.

"Say my name, Emma," he commands, his breath hot on my neck. "Let everyone know who you belong to."

"Kirill!" I scream, my climax washing over me like a tidal wave, obliterating everything in its path. He follows suit, his own orgasm ripping through him as he fills me with his warmth.

Kirill has awakened a fire inside me that I never knew existed – and I'm not sure if I ever want it to be extinguished.

I lounge on the plush sofa, absently flipping through a glossy magazine. Boredom gnaws at me like an insistent itch I can't quite reach. The pictures blur together as my mind wanders, craving excitement and adventure in this new world that still feels so foreign to me.

The door swings open, revealing Natasha. She saunters over with a grin, her confident stride a testament to her power in this male-dominated realm. It's hard not to admire her.

"Natasha," I greet her. "What brings you here today?".

Her eyes scan the room briefly before focusing on me. "I have a special surprise for you," she says with a mischievous glimmer in her eyes. "Kirill sent me to take you for a pampering session. Mani-pedi, massage, just the two of us."

My eyes light up at the prospect of pampering. It's a nice distraction from the swirling uncertainty that's become my life.

"Oh, that's so sweet of him! I could use some relaxation. Just a minute."

As we make our way toward the door, the sound of muffled voices drifts through the open windows. I don't know why but pause. I overhear two servants gossiping. They think they're being discreet, but their disdain is palpable. I catch my name and feel my heart clench.

"I saw her with that Victor earlier. Kissing him on the cheek like it's nothing!" one of the servants scoff.

"Yeah, she's nothing but a slut. Kirill should never have married someone like her. She doesn't belong here."

Rage boils inside me, but it's mingled with a sickening sense of inadequacy. Am I truly so unwelcome in this world I was born into? I may be loyal to the mafia, but it seems loyalty isn't enough. I look fearfully at Natasha wondering what she might be thinking.

Victor is my friend and has come to visit me. We haven't seen each other since the wedding. He just wanted to make sure I was okay. Not that there's anything he could do if I wasn't. I'm not one of them anymore.

I don't think I can fit in. I'll always be an outsider.

Do they think I didn't notice their disdainful looks? Their whispering behind my back? The little nudges: lukewarm coffee in the morning, cold meal when Kirill's not around. Yet I haven't said anything because I don't want to make a fuss.

Before I can react, Natasha whirls around, her eyes blazing with fury. She marches over to the windows, throwing them open wide. The servants freeze in surprise, their faces pale as they realize they have been overheard.

THE PRICE OF POWER

"What did you just say?" Natasha's voice is ice-cold, cutting through the air like a whip.

The servants stammer, their faces turning red with embarrassment.

Natasha's voice is sharp and commanding. "Let me make something very clear to both of you. Emma is a woman of integrity and strength. She is respected and loved by Kirill, and her actions are none of your business. It is not your place to judge her or anyone else for that matter. I wonder what Kirill will say about this."

The servants pale of the mention of Kirill. They mumble apologies.

I reach out and touch Natasha's arm. "Thank you, Natasha. You have no idea how much it means to me that you stood up for me."

Natasha's stern expression softens, a warm smile gracing her lips. "Of course, Emma. We're family now, and I won't let anyone disrespect my family. Let's forget about those ignorant remarks and focus on enjoying our pampering session. Kirill wants you to feel loved and cherished, and that's exactly what you deserve."

After a twenty minutes ride we enter the luxurious salon. The air is filled with the soothing aroma of scented candles and fragrant oils. Soft instrumental music plays in the background. The walls are adorned with elegant artwork, and plush chairs lined the room. The staff moves gracefully, attending to their clients with meticulous care.

At first, we are led to a separate room with two massage beds. Two middle-aged women tuck us in after we undress and lie down on the bed. As one of them starts massaging me with lavender-scented oil, I forget everything. I really needed this. I groan as she reaches a particularly painful lump. This is very good. I'm not even going to get up from here.

After one hour the masseurs leave us alone. I turn my attention to Natasha, I want to know her.

"So, Natasha," I begin. "Tell me more about your position in the organization. What exactly do you do?"

She smiles, pride shining in her eyes. "I'm responsible for the digital operations. My skills as a hacker and my knowledge of cybersecurity have proven to be invaluable. We've realized the potential of the digital world in expanding our reach and protecting our interests."

I nod, impressed by Natasha's expertise and the innovative approach they are taking. "That's incredible. It shows how adaptable and forward-thinking the organization is becoming."

Natasha's smile fades slightly as she continues, her voice tinged with a hint of melancholy. "You know, it wasn't always like this. My father was strict and ruthless. He expected a son to continue his legacy, but instead, he got me, his only daughter. He resented that fact."

I understand that. In the mafia, women don't count, only men. "I'm sorry you had to go through that, Natasha. It must have been challenging to break free from those expectations."

Natasha nods, her gaze distant. "It was, but it also made me stronger. I refused to be limited by their traditional notions. I proved that I could be just as valuable, if not more, in this world."

I admire Natasha. It must not have been easy. These roads are not paved with stones but with minefields.

"What about Kirill's father?" I ask. "I've heard rumors about him being ruthless, even demonic."

Her expression darkens, a shadow crossing her features. "Those rumors are not entirely unfounded. Kirill's father, Vladimir, was a formidable figure in the underworld."

I lean closer. "And Kirill? What was his relationship like with his father?"

"It is not for me to say. You have to ask Kirill."

"I've heard rumors, Natasha. About the things Kirill has done, the power he wields. It frightens me."

Natasha nods, her expression filled with empathy. "I won't deny that Kirill is a complex man, shaped by his past and the expectations placed upon him. But there's another side to him, Emma. A side that few people get to see."

This piques my curiosity. "And what is that?"

Natasha smiled faintly. "A desire for change. Kirill wants to take the organization in a new direction. He sees potential beyond the traditional ways. And he wants to protect those he cares about, even if it means making difficult choices."

I mull over Natasha's words.

Natasha reaches out and gently places her hand on mine. "We're both in this together, Emma. We may have different roles within the organization, but we share a common struggle. And maybe, just maybe, we can find strength in each other."

I look into Natasha's eyes, recognizing a newfound connection between us.

Maybe... Maybe we can be friends.

Chapter 7

Kirill

The rain pours outside, a fitting backdrop for the meeting I've called tonight. My captains gather around the long mahogany table, their eyes fix on me as I walk to the head of the room. I clear my throat, preparing to reveal my plans.

"Times are changing," I begin, commanding the attention of everyone present. "Tonight, we embrace a new era for Diabol. We're stepping away from our traditional ways and entering the digital age." Murmurs echo through the room, and I continue without pause. "We can no longer rely on the old ways if we want to stay ahead of our enemies. We must adapt, and that means embracing technology."

I glance over at Natasha, her slender fingers dancing across her laptop keyboard. She nods at me, her gray eyes filled with determination. She's been my rock throughout this transition, and I trust her implicitly.

"Natasha will demonstrate one of our new programs," I say, gesturing to the large screen behind me. The room darkens as she brings up a complex web of code. "She has been working tirelessly to implement these changes.

"Every single transaction made by our rivals will be recorded, analyzed, and exploited," Natasha explains, her voice steady despite the weight of the room's attention. "We'll know when they make deals, who they're working with, and how much money is changing hands. This information will give us unparalleled power over them."

"Isn't this too risky?" Dimitri, an older member with graying hair and a permanent scowl, finally speaks up. "What if they catch us spying on them?"

"Ah," I say, smirking devilishly. "That's where the beauty of this program lies. Once we've extracted the information we need, it erases all traces of our presence, leaving no indication that we were ever there."

As Natasha continues detailing our technological advancements, I watch my people carefully. Some are still hesitant, but others lean forward in their seats, their eyes alight with excitement. This is what we need – to evolve, to adapt, to conquer.

Some of my men exchange furtive glances, their unease palpable even from a distance.

"Speak up," I command. "If you have concerns, air them now."

"Kirill," Alexis begins, nervously twisting his hands. "We understand your desire to modernize and use technology, but some of us... well, we worry about losing our traditional ways. We don't want to abandon the old path entirely - the drugs, the girls... it's what we know."

I study their faces, the anxiety in their eyes mixed with a stubborn refusal to change. A part of me understands their reluctance; our organization has thrived on these methods for decades. But progress cannot be halted.

"Listen to me," I say firmly, holding their gaze. "We are not eradicating our past. The drugs, the girls - they will still have their place. But by embracing the digital world, we will have greater power and influence than ever before. Trust me. Our core values remain unchanged. We will continue to honor and protect our own, and we will never shy away from the necessary violence to maintain our position. However," I add, my voice taking on a harder edge, "we will not be left behind as our enemies grow stronger. We must embrace this change or risk becoming obsolete. I expect each of you to embrace these changes."

The dark room is heavy with tension, but I feel a spark of hope flickering within me. They may resist at first, but they'll come around eventually.

"Dismissed," I say, watching as they file out of the room.

As the door closes behind the last of them, I turn to Natasha and nod, a silent gesture of gratitude. She returns the nod and shifts her focus back to her laptop, her fingers resuming their rapid dance across the keys.

"Let's get to work."

Later that afternoon, I arrive at Luke's office, my jaw clenched tight as I recall the disturbing image of Victor kissing Emma. My Emma. The anger radiates from my body as I stride into the room, my presence filling the space and causing Luke and Victor's laughter to die instantly. They jump up from the table. Their expressions shift from amusement to wariness, sensing the storm that has entered the room.

Alliance or not, there are lines that should never be crossed.

"Victor!" I bellow, my voice laced with a potent mix of fury and accusation. My eyes bore into him. Luke's eyes dart back and forth between Victor and me.

"What brings you here, Kirill?" Luke asks, his voice carefully measured.

"Cut the bullshit," I snap, my words slicing through the air like a whip. The room becomes charged with electric energy as I confront Victor directly. "Why the hell were you kissing my wife?"

Victor's face pales as my words hit him with the force of a sucker punch. He stumbles over his words, desperately searching for an excuse.

"Kirill, calm down," Luke interjects, his tone tinged with concern.

"Calm down?!" I scoff, my voice dripping with sarcasm. "Tell your lapdog to keep his filthy paws off my wife, and we can talk about calm."

Victor's eyes dart nervously between Luke and me, clearly uncomfortable under the weight of my anger. He tries to regain his composure, a hint of defiance creeping into his voice. "Emma and I were just having a friendly moment, Kirill," Victor insists, his voice strained. "We have been friends for years. You're overreacting."

My anger bubbles to the surface, fueled by a possessiveness that cannot be contained. The muscles in my fists tighten, causing my knuckles to turn white as I hold myself back from unleashing the full force of my fury. A dark smile plays at the corner of my lips as I take a step closer, invading his personal space, my gaze locked with his.

"Let me make this clear, Victor," I growl. "Emma is mine, and no one else's. She is off-limits to you and anyone else who dares to cross that line..."

THE PRICE OF POWER

Victor's bravado falters, his confidence crumbling under the weight of my unwavering determination. He stammers, his words stumbling over one another.

"I-I didn't mean any harm, Kirill," he stammers. "I apologize."

"Emma is mine," I growl. Every syllable is punctuated by the unwavering conviction of my claim. "Alliance or not, you do not touch her. Understood? Remember your place, Victor, or you'll find yourself in a position you won't enjoy."

He nods slowly, a mix of fear and remorse etched on his face. The weight of my words hangs heavy in the air, the unspoken threat of consequences lingering beneath the surface.

"Enough, both of you," Luke interjects. "This rivalry is getting out of hand. We need to focus on our common goals."

I narrow my eyes at Luke, a cold smile curving my lips. "You're right, Luke. We do have common goals. But remember, I won't tolerate anyone disrespecting what's mine."

Luke's gaze meets mine, his expression cautious but resolute. "I understand, Kirill. Let's put this behind us and move forward."

With a curt nod, I turn on my heel, my gaze lingering on Victor for a moment longer before exiting the room.

The door slams shut behind me, reverberating with the force of my departure.

As I make my way down the corridor, my thoughts consumed by Emma, I can't shake the possessive fire burning within me. The lines have been drawn, and I am determined to protect what is rightfully mine.

The door slams behind me as I enter the house, my pulse still racing from confronting Victor. Emma is in the living room, curled up on the couch with a book. She glances over at me with a mixture of surprise and curiosity.

"Kirill, you're home early," she says, setting down her book. "How was your day?"

"Fine," I mutter, my eyes fixed on her. "You seemed to enjoy your massage."

"Thank you, it was lovely," she replies, smiling. "Just what I needed after the past few days."

"Did anything else happen today?" I probe, my voice tense. "Any visitors?"

She hesitates, but then shakes her head. "No, just a quiet day at home."

"Really? No friends stopping by? Like Victor?" I press, my anger bubbling up again.

Emma's eyes widen in surprise, her cheeks flushing red. "Victor was here...but it was nothing, Kirill. He just wanted to check up on me. He was curious if everything was okay with me."

"Is that all?" I demand, stepping closer to her. "He had no other reason to come here?"

"None that I know of," she frowns. "Why are you being so aggressive, Kirill? It's not like Victor did anything wrong."

"Wrong?" I laugh bitterly. "I caught him kissing you, Emma. That's more than wrong."

Her eyes grow wide, and she struggles for a moment before regaining her composure. "You caught? How..? Kirill, it wasn't like that. It was just a friendly kiss on the cheek. You're overreacting."

THE PRICE OF POWER

"Overreacting?" My hands grip her shoulders tightly, my face inches from hers. "He touched you, Emma. No one touches what's mine."

"Yours?" She pushes me away, anger sparking in her eyes. "I'm not some possession, Kirill. And maybe you should trust me to handle my own friendships."

"Trust?" I snarl, my jealousy consuming me. "How can I trust you when you're keeping secrets?"

"Fine," she spits back, her own fury rising to meet mine. "You want the truth? Yes, Victor kissed me. But it was on the cheek, and it meant nothing. You're turning this into something it's not."

"Am I?" I challenge, leaning in close again, our bodies nearly touching. "Prove it."

"Prove it?" Emma repeats, her voice shaky but defiant. "How am I supposed to prove that to you?"

"Show me," I growl, my hands reaching for her waist. "Show me that you belong to me."

Her breath catches as I pull her against me, our lips crashing together in a passionate, angry kiss.

"Kirill..." she gasps as I lift her into my arms, carrying her toward the bedroom. Our clothes are discarded hastily, our touches rough and demanding, as if trying to stake our claims on one another.

"Kirill..." she moans softly as my mouth envelopes her breast, my teeth grazing her nipple as my tongue flicks it teasingly. Her body arches into me, seeking more of my touch.

"Tell me what you want," I demand huskily, my voice barely audible above the raggedness of our breathing.

"Take me, Kirill. I need to feel you inside me."

"Then say it," I command, my gaze locked onto hers as I position myself at her entrance. "Tell me you belong to me."

"I...I belong to you, Kirill," she whispers, her eyes filled with a mix of defiance and need. "Please," she whispers, her voice barely audible.

With a final, possessive thrust, I claim her, our bodies moving together in a primal dance of desire. And even as we reach our peak, our connection forged through anger and jealousy, I can't help but feel a twisted sense of satisfaction.

Emma is mine and mine alone.

Chapter 8
Emma

I sit next to Natasha, our shoulders almost touching as we hunch over the laptop screen. The glow of the monitor casts a faint light on her determined expression, accentuating the intensity in her eyes. I watch her every move, captivated by her skill and expertise.

"Okay, Emma, now you need to bypass the firewall like this," she explains, her fingers dancing gracefully across the keyboard. I watch intently, feeling a thrill at the prospect of learning something that could make me more valuable to the organization. I want to contribute, to be seen as more than just a pretty face.

"Got it," I say, mimicking her movements and surprising myself with how naturally it comes to me. A small smile tugs at the corner of my lips, and I can see the pride reflected in Natasha's eyes.

"Wow, you're picking this up really quickly," she says. "I knew you had it in you."

"Thanks, Natasha," I reply, blushing slightly at her praise.

Our friendship has grown stronger over time, and I'm grateful for the bond we share. In this dark, male-dominated world, it's comforting to know I have someone like her by my side.

Our fingers fly across the keyboards, the soft clicking noise filling the room as we dive deeper into the web. It feels empowering like I'm tapping into a secret part of the universe, one that only a select few can access. And as I glance over at Natasha, I realize that she must feel it too.

"Natasha, do you ever wonder what our lives would be like if we hadn't been born into this world? If we were free to choose our own paths?" I ask, curiosity gnawing at me.

She pauses for a moment, her fingers hovering above the keys as she considers my question. "Sometimes," she admits, her gaze drifting toward the window. "But then I remember that this is the life we were given, and we have to make the best of it. We can't change our past, but we can shape our future."

"True," I agree, my thoughts turning to my own family and the expectations placed upon me. I'm not sure if I can ever truly escape this world, but at least with Natasha by my side, I know I won't have to face it alone.

"Alright, back to work," she says, snapping me out of my reverie. "We've got a lot more to cover."

I look up from the laptop as Kirill enters the room, his commanding presence instantly drawing my attention. He leans against the doorway, a smirk playing on his lips as he takes in the scene before him.

"Who would have thought I'd have two such clever women working for me?" he teases, his eyes locked onto mine with an intensity that sends shivers down my spine. "It's almost unfair to our enemies."

"Almost," Natasha agrees with a grin, her fingers still dancing across the keyboard.

Suddenly, the laptop screen vibrates, and an alarm blares throughout the room.

THE PRICE OF POWER

My heart races as I try to process what's happening. Natasha's fingers fly even faster over the keys, her face contorts in concentration. "We're being cyberattacked," she announces, her voice tense.

"By whom?" Kirill demands, his eyes narrowing.

"Looks like it's an MC gang... The Savage Sons," Natasha replies, her voice strained as she works to counter the attack.

"Dammit!" Kirill curses, slamming his fist against the wall. He strides over to the table where we sit, his gaze fixes on the screen. "What's our plan?"

I watch as Natasha types furiously, her fingers a blur above the keyboard. She pauses momentarily, turning her gaze to Kirill. "We need to launch a counterattack, but it has to be precise. We don't want to risk alerting them."

"Agreed," Kirill says, his voice cold. "Emma, watch Natasha and learn. I'll coordinate our other resources."

"Of course, Kirill," I reply. It's terrifying, but also thrilling, to be involved in the inner workings of his organization.

I turn my attention back to the screen.

"Almost there," Natasha mutters, her eyes never leaving the screen. "Just a few more adjustments..."

"Good," Kirill says, his jaw clenches. "Once this is over, we'll make sure The Savage Sons regrets ever crossing us."

A dangerous glint appears in his eyes, and my body responds instinctively to the raw power he exudes. Even in the face of danger, I find myself drawn to him, caught up in this magnetic pull that seems to exist between us.

"Got it! I'm ready!" Natasha looks around with sparkling eyes. "They didn't stand a chance."

"Let's go out for dinner, and celebrate our small victory," Kirill suggests, his eyes twinkling with mischief. "We deserve it."

"Sounds good to me," Natasha agrees, stretching her arms above her head after hours spent hunched over her laptop.

"Emma?" Kirill turns to me, a devilish grin on his face that I can't resist.

"Alright, let's do it," I concede, my heart racing at the prospect of spending more time with him.

The restaurant is modern and elegant, the soft glow of candles casting flickering shadows against the walls. As we settle into our seats and peruse the menu, I feel the warmth of Kirill's presence beside me, his knee brushing against mine under the table.

"Try the steak," he advises, his deep voice always sends shivers down my spine. "It's their specialty."

"Thanks for the tip," I reply, trying to keep my voice steady.

I order the steak as recommended, while Kirill and Natasha opt for pasta dishes. As we wait for our food, we chat about everything from childhood memories to current events, the conversation flowing easily between us. It's a rare moment of normalcy in our otherwise chaotic lives, and I relish every second of it.

As we step outside the restaurant, the pleasantly cool air hits my face.

"Stay close, Emma," Kirill murmurs into my ear, his hot breath stirring my hair. He pulls me in tighter, and I feel the reassuring weight of his arm around me.

THE PRICE OF POWER

"Kirill, I..." My words are cut short as gunshots suddenly ring out. Panic surges through my veins, quickening my heartbeat as adrenaline courses through my body.

Figures in black dresses emerge from the shadows, their menacing presence casting a sinister aura. Their intent is clear, and my instincts scream at me to find safety. But before I can react, Kirill's voice cuts through the chaos, commanding and urgent.

"Get down!" he orders. Without hesitation, he grabs hold of me, guiding me behind the shelter of a nearby car. The metal is cold against my back as I crouch down, seeking cover.

The world around us transforms into a battlefield, filled with flashes of gunfire and the echoes of destruction. Innocent bystanders become unwitting casualties caught in the crossfire, their terrified screams piercing the night.

My heart races, fear consuming me. My gaze darts around, taking in the chaotic scene before me. Shadows dance and flicker, blending with the disarray of the night. The flickering streetlights cast eerie, disjointed shadows on the pavement.

Kirill's eyes, once filled with warmth and tenderness, now burn with fire.

"Natasha, cover us!" Kirill shouts, holding his own weapon. She nods and returns fire, her face a picture of fierce determination.

Fear threatens to overwhelm me, but I draw upon every ounce of courage within me, refusing to let it consume me completely.

"Emma, stay with me," Kirill pleads, his gaze locked on mine for a moment.

Through the cacophony of gunshots and cries, I spot a figure taking aim at Kirill from behind. My heart lurches in my chest, its rhythm disrupted by a surge of adrenaline and a surge of sheer terror. Time seems to slow as my instincts kick into overdrive. Without a second thought, I throw myself in front of Kirill.

Pain sears through my arm as a bullet tears through the flesh. An anguished cry escapes my lips.

"Emma!" Kirill catches me before I hit the ground, cradling me in his strong arms. Blood pours from my wound, staining his hands and the pavement below.

"Kirill, I couldn't let them..." I gasp, trying to convey my desperate need to protect him.

He presses his lips against my forehead. "Never do that again! You can't jump in front of a bullet. Oh, my God, Emma. I couldn't stand it if anything happened to you."

Kirill and Natasha defend our position as more people try to close in on us.

"Emma, hold on," Kirill's voice breaks through the haze.

I cling to him, feeling the heat of his body.

Gritting my teeth, I fight against the dizziness threatening to engulf me. I can't afford to give in to weakness, not now, not when they're so close.

"I'm... I'm fine," I manage to gasp, my voice strained. "Keep... keep fighting."

Natasha positions herself beside me, her gaze scanning my arm. When she touches the wound, I hiss. "Everything is okay, the bullet just brushed you." She takes off her coat. "Here, press on it."

THE PRICE OF POWER

As the battle wages on, I find the strength to push myself up, using the nearby car for support. My injured arm throbs, but I force myself to ignore the pain.

When the number of shots seems to be decreasing, we retreat from the battleground. Kirill wraps his arm around my waist, providing support as we make a mad dash toward our car.

Every step sends a jolt of agony through my body, but I refuse to let it slow me down.

"Almost there, Emma," Kirill's voice is laced with concern, his grip tightening around me. "Hold on, we're going to get you home."

I nod, my breath coming in ragged gasps, my eyes locked on our vehicle just a few yards away.

As we reach the car, Natasha is already at the driver's side, her eyes focused. She unlocks the doors with a swift motion, the clicking sound bringing a surge of relief. Kirill guides me into the backseat, his touch gentle yet urgent.

"I'm worried about the shot," Kirill admits, his voice heavy with concern. "We need to get you to our doc, Emma."

I wince as pain shoots through my arm, but I summon a brave smile. "It's just a scratch, Kirill. I'll be fine. We have to keep going."

Natasha slides into the driver's seat, her gaze flickering between Kirill and me in the rearview mirror.

"This is her initiation, Kirill," she says, her voice calm but resolute. "Emma's proving herself to the family, to the organization."

Kirill's brow furrows, worry etched across his face. "Initiation or not, she's hurt. We can't ignore that."

I interject. "Kirill, I can handle this. I'm stronger than you think."

He meets my gaze, his eyes searching for any sign of doubt.

I lean back in the seat, my injured arm cradled against my chest, my gaze fixed on the city lights passing by.

Kirill's hand finds mine, his touch offering both comfort and strength. I squeeze his hand, silently reassuring him that I'm okay.

"We'll be home soon," Natasha says, her voice carrying exhaustion. "You know they were the Savage Sons, right? I saw two of them had tattoos on the back of their hands. Two snakes."

"Those goddamn bastards! I swear, I'll make them pay for what they've done. No one hurts Emma and gets away with it! They don't know who they're dealing with. They'll curse the day they were born."

As we make our way back to our apartment, my mind races with thoughts of what just happened. I've seen firsthand the damage this lifestyle can cause. The scenes of violence and destruction replay in my mind.

"Are you alright?" Kirill asks me gently once we're home, alone. His gaze searches mine, trying to gauge the depths of my fear and uncertainty.

I nod, avoiding his gaze, not wanting to reveal the flicker of doubt that dances in my eyes.

"Sit on the bed. I'll be right back with a wet cloth, disinfectant, and bandages," Kirill instructs. I watch him leave the room, and as soon as the door closes, I allow myself a moment of vulnerability. The weight of the situation crashes over me, and I let out a loud, shuddering sigh, releasing some of the tension that has built up inside me.

Is this the life I truly want? The mafia, the power struggles... the collateral damage caused by our actions? The questions swirl in my mind, threatening to consume me. But before I can dwell on them further, Kirill returns.

"May I?" he asks. Gently, he takes the bloody piece of cloth still clutched in my hand, his touch both gentle and firm. As he begins to clean the wound, a stinging sensation courses through me, a reminder of the dangers we face.

"I'm sorry. I'm sorry this could have happened to you," Kirill murmurs, his voice tinged with regret. "I promised I'd always protect you." His words tug at my heart, and I reach out to touch his hand, offering solace.

"It's not your fault," I assure him. "I'm glad it wasn't more serious."

Kirill releases a heavy breath and gently brings his forehead to mine. "Emma, I see the turmoil in your eyes. What troubles you?"

"Kirill, I've witnessed the pain inflicted upon those who have no part in our world. The collateral damage cuts deep, and I can't help but question the price we pay for power and control."

Kirill tenderly intertwines his fingers with mine, and murmurs. "I understand, my love. But we must also remember that the world we inhabit is one of shadows and secrets. Our actions, however ruthless they may seem, are often driven by a desire to protect what matters most to us.

"And what about the people we hurt along the way? The ones who suffer because of our decisions?" I search his eyes as I speak.

A contemplative pause lingers between us as Kirill carefully selects his words, knowing the gravity of his response. "We strive for balance, Emma. We do what we can to minimize the damage, to shield the innocent. But we can't always control the consequences of our choices."

"It's a heavy burden to bear, Kirill. Sometimes I wonder if we're doing more harm than good."

Kirill's gaze softens and he pulls me closer. "We can't change the past, Emma, but we can learn from it. We can strive to make a difference, to create a better future for those we care about. I work for a better future with you."

"But at what cost? So much bloodshed, lives lost... Is this the price we have to pay for power and control?"

"Emma, every choice we make comes with consequences. We knew the risks when we entered this world. But we also have the ability to shape its course, to bring order amidst chaos."

Kirill stands up and offers his hand. I put my still shaking hand in it and he carefully stands me up. He turns me around and pulls down the zipper of my dress.

"I don't want to lose sight of our humanity, Kirill. We must remember the lives affected by our actions, both within our organization and beyond."

When the dress folds around my ankles, Kirill turns me back and nods, looking deep into my eyes. "You're right, my love. This should serve as a reminder of the responsibility we carry. We must use our power wisely, to protect, not destroy."

I take a deep breath. "Let's rebuild, Kirill. Let's create a foundation where our organization can flourish without compromising our values. We can be a force for good in this dark world."

"I couldn't agree more, Emma. We'll forge a path that merges strength with compassion, power with empathy. Our family will be a sanctuary, a place where honor and loyalty reign supreme."

Kirill lifts the blanket and I dutifully lie down. "Together, we'll navigate the complexities of our dark and dangerous world. We'll make amends for the sacrifices made, and ensure that our legacy is one of redemption and hope."

Kirill provides a glass of water with a pill. "Take it, it's a painkiller."

"Thank you." My eyes grow heavy with exhaustion. I envision a future where strife and chaos cease to exist. In the world of dreams, endless possibilities exist, and it is there that the seeds of change are sown.

Chapter 9

Kirill

The amber glow of Vlad's cigar burns brightly in my office. The smell of tobacco fills the room. I don't smoke, but I like the smell, which is why I let Vlad do it.

"Kirill," Natasha's voice breaks through my thoughts. She sits at her computer, long, slender fingers tapping away at the keyboard, her dark hair cascading over her shoulders. "We've tracked them down to several locations in the city."

"Good," I say, taking my eyes off the glowing embers and turning to Natasha, feeling my chest tighten with the weight of my anger and concern. Emma's face flashes through my mind – beautiful, delicate, and wounded. I can't let her get hurt again; not by the Savage Sons or anyone else.

Vlad leans back in his chair in front of my table, his tattooed arms crossed over his chest, his expression hard and determined. As my Enforcer, he is ruthless and efficient.

"Let's go over the plan," I say. "I want to hit them where it hurts, and I want to do it now."

"Of course, Kirill." Natasha nods, her green eyes reflecting the glow from her computer screen. "Our best option is to take out their main weapons cache. It's heavily guarded, but if we can blow it up, it'll send a clear message that we won't be pushed around."

"Agreed," Vlad rumbles, cracking his knuckles. "I'll round up some men, and we'll take care of it tonight."

"Make sure you're prepared for anything," I warn him. "These bastards have already proven they're willing to play dirty."

"Understood," Vlad replies with a nod.

"Good." I turn to Natasha. "And you? What else have you found?"

"Several of their key members are meeting tonight at an underground club," she says, her fingers still flying across the keyboard. "It might be worth infiltrating and listening in on their conversation."

"Excellent idea, but I want you to stay here and monitor the situation from a distance. Your hacking skills will be invaluable if things go south."

"Understood, Kirill," she says, her eyes never leaving the screen.

"Vlad, what about Maxim? Is he still on our payroll? I want him to get close enough to hear what they're saying. I trust you can handle that?"

"Of course," he grins, revealing his sharp, predatory teeth. "He was born for this. I'll call him."

"Then it's settled," I say, clenching my fists at my sides, feeling the heat of revenge coursing through my veins. "We strike tonight, and we don't stop until they're brought to its knees."

Natasha and Vlad exchange a glance, a shared understanding passing between them. They know the stakes, the risks involved, and yet they stand by me without hesitation. Their loyalty means everything to me, especially now when Emma's safety hangs in the balance.

"Let's do this. Let's make them regret the day they crossed us," I say. "Let's make them pay for hurting Emma."

"Agreed," they echo in unison, and we set to work.

As we finalize our plans, I can't help but think of Emma – her soft skin, her intoxicating scent, the way she looks when she's lost in pleasure beneath me like yesterday evening.

I'd do anything to keep her safe, to protect her from the darkness that surrounds us. And if that means waging war on the Mc Gang, then so be it.

Tonight, there will be bloodshed, pain, and chaos, but it's a price I'm willing to pay for the woman I've come to care for more than I ever thought possible.

As we discuss the best course of action to take against the MC Gang, my eyes keep darting to the screen on my laptop, where I have a live feed of my apartment. My heart aches with longing and concern as I watch Emma moving around.

I watch her every movement, admiring the way her body sways, her hips teasing me with their sensual rhythm.

I know it's wrong to let my mind wander to such dark, erotic thoughts when we're in the midst of planning a war, but I can't help myself.

"Kirill," Vlad interrupts my thoughts, "focus."

"Right, right. Sorry," I mutter, tearing my gaze away from Emma for a moment. We continue discussing strategies, but my attention remains divided between the conversation at hand and the entrancing beauty on the screen.

The next moment I look at the screen, I notice something odd happening in the footage – the front door of the apartment is being forced open. A surge of panic courses through me, followed by an all-consuming rage. I'm unable to tear my eyes from the screen as two masked men enter, guns drawn.

"No," I shout. I jump up from my chair.

A thousand thoughts race through my mind, but one thought blazes above all others - I must reach Emma, I must save her.

"Natasha, Vlad, we've got to move," I growl. Without hesitation, we spring into action, their eyes fix on the laptop screen, mirroring my frantic gaze.

"What the fuck?" growls Vlad.

We rush towards the door, and I snatch my laptop, unwilling to lose sight of Emma's peril even for a moment. We storm out of the apartment.

With Natasha and Vlad in tow, I sprint toward my car parked nearby. My hands tremble as I fumble with the keys, my mind consumed by a desperate need to reach Emma's side.

Every second that passes feels like an eternity, the fear for her safety gnawing at my core.

Natasha snatches it from my hand and gets into the driver's seat. Vlad sits next to me in the back.

Finally, the engine roars to life.

My grip on the laptop tightens until my knuckles turn white. My eyes remain fixed on the screen, the flickering images of Emma's struggle etched into my mind. I watch helplessly as she fights with every ounce of her being, her determination shining through despite the overwhelming odds.

But then, a sickening blow lands, and Emma crumples to the ground, unconscious. My heart sinks, terror and rage surging through me.

One of the figures finally turns fully toward the camera and gives a sinister grin.

"Jurij!" I spat. "You will pay for this betrayal. You are a dead man," I seethe.

Jurij's actions have ignited a fire within me, a fire that will not be quelled until justice is served.

With every fiber of my being, I vow to save Emma, to make those responsible for her suffering pay the highest price.

"Check the cameras outside the building," Natasha suggests. "Maybe we can get a better look at their getaway vehicle."

"Good idea," I nod, hastily switching feeds and scanning the footage. Sure enough, we catch a glimpse of a black SUV speeding away from the scene. The license plate is obscured, but it's a start.

"Send this to our loyal members," I order Vlad. "Tell them to let me know immediately if they spot it."

"Got it," he replies, already on his phone relaying the information.

"Natasha, you and I will scour the city," I say. "We'll find Emma, and we'll make these fuckers pay for what they've done."

"Agreed," she says. "Let's go."

I don't bother going into my apartment.

We drop Vlad out by one of our bars and Natasha and I circle the city. My mind is consumed by thoughts of Emma – her warm embrace, her delicate touch, the way she looks up at me with those wide, innocent eyes.

They took her from me, and I won't rest until I have her back – and until Jurij and all those who chose him are nothing but a memory.

The darkness within me threatens to consume me whole, but I know there's no turning back now. It's time to wage war, and may God have mercy on their souls, because I certainly won't.

The night is dark and cold, but my anger burns hot as we speed through the city streets. It has been three days and still no clue where they have taken her.

Fuck!

I can't shake the image of Emma's battered face from my mind; it fuels my rage, driving me to take extreme measures in order to find her.

"Vlad, how many people are on our list?" I ask, gripping the steering wheel tightly.

"Six," he replies, scrolling through his phone. "All possible leads who might know something about Jurij's whereabouts."

"Good. Who to start with?" I ask.

"Haasan. He's always at Raw at this time."

Raw is a shitty bar on the outskirts of town I wouldn't normally set foot in.

I shudder.

We gotta find something.

We arrive at the location – the dingy bar frequented by criminals and lowlifes. As we walk in, the atmosphere turns tense, and all eyes are on us.

I don't care. Let them stare. Let them fear me.

Vlad points to a dark corner. "There."

I approach the man sitting alone. He looks nervous even in his drunken state, as he takes me in.

"Evening," I greet him, taking a seat opposite him without waiting for an invitation. "You seem like a man who knows things. Tell me, have you heard anything about Jurij Kozlov or where he hides?"

"Wh-what? I don't know whom you're talking about," he stammers, clearly lying as he touches his nose and averts his gaze.

"Wrong answer," I growl, grabbing his hand and twisting it painfully behind his back. "I suggest you start talking, or things will get much worse for you."

"O-okay, okay!" he cries, tears streaming down his face. "I heard him bragging about that he's going to rise to a high position because he's going to force you on your knees. He has the means."

"Has he? And what is that tool?" I ask in a calm voice, however, my nerves are about to explode.

"I...I dunno."

"Where is he?" I demand, applying more pressure to his arm.

"I don't know. I really don't know," he sobs. "But there is an old warehouse down by the docks," he whimpers. "I often see him there with his brother."

"Thank you," I say, releasing him with a shove. "You just saved your own life."

I beckon Natasha and Vlad over, quickly filling them in on what I've learned. We waste no time heading to the warehouse.

We easily find it. There's no movement in front of it, and everything around it is dark. I motion with my head for Vlad to go ahead. He nods in understanding, his eyes focused and alert. He moves forward with measured steps, leading the way toward the entrance. Natasha and I follow closely behind, our guns held firmly in our hands. The warehouse is dark and reeks of decay as we enter. I raise my hand, signaling Vlad to halt just in front of the door. We pause for a moment, scanning the area for any hidden threats or signs of activity. I motion with a subtle nod for Vlad to proceed. Natasha and I follow him, our senses heightened, and our focus razor-sharp.

One of the interior spaces resounds with laughter. We approach cautiously. In the doorless space stay a tall and imposing figure.

"He is Jurij's brother, Andrei," Natasha gapes.

Hiding behind the pallets of goods, I slowly creep closer. He doesn't suspect a thing, he's on the phone talking about the delivery of the stuff. Reaching behind him, I shut his mouth and throw his phone on the floor. Natasha steps on it, smashing it to pieces.

He's struggling to get free, but he can't fight me off. Vlad ties his hands with a rope and tapes his mouth shut.

"Let's go to our torture chamber."

The drive is short, but it doesn't feel like it.

All my thoughts are about Emma.

I'm going crazy.

Just don't let anything happen to her.

I'm starting to get a sense of what Luke was going through when my father kidnapped Gaby. This helplessness is eating me up.

I hang Andrei from a rope in the basement of my office building. His toe barely touches the concrete. I rip the tape off his mouth. "Talk," I bark.

"Go to hell," he spits.

"Wrong answer," I say, taking out a knife and pressing it against his cheek. "How about I start by carving off your face?"

"Alright, alright!" he yells, fear finally breaking through his facade. "What do you want to know?"

"Where can we find her?" Natasha asks.

"Her?"

"I think you're playing with me." I make a sharp cut across his chest. But I'm not stopping here. I make a deep cut on his arm too, then on his face from his eyebrows to his chin. His cry is music to my ears. "Want to reconsider your answer?"

"Yes! Please, don't hurt me anymore."

"Last chance. Talk."

"He bought an old mansion on the outskirts of the city, he is holding your wife hostage there," he confesses. "But you'll never get in – it's heavily guarded."

"We'll see about that," I say, my eyes narrowing. "What's the address?"

He quickly blurts out, tears running down his face. I don't need to write it down, it burns in my brain.

"Thank you for your cooperation."

I'm heading for the door, I need to get there as soon as possible.

"Boss, what do we do with him?" Vlad asks.

"Kill him," I order, my voice devoid of mercy. "But let his death be slow."

"Understood," Vlad says without hesitation.

I don't have time for this now.

I'm coming Emma. Hang on, I'll be right there.

Chapter 10

Emma

The cold, damp air of the mansion's basement crawls across my skin like a thousand tiny insects. I'm bound to a rickety wooden chair, my legs shaking uncontrollably as I try to process the events that led me here. The dim lightbulb hanging overhead flickers.

"Look at you, Emma," Jurij sneers, pacing in front of me with his hands clasped behind his back. "Pathetic."

"Please," I whimper, trying to swallow the lump in my throat. My voice trembles and I know he can sense my fear. "Why are you doing this?"

"Because you're in the way, and I hate you," he growls, stopping in front of me and grabbing my chin roughly. His icy blue eyes pierce into mine, sending shivers down my spine. "You don't deserve Kirill. You don't deserve to be a pakhan's wife. You are just an Italian whore. You're nothing but a pretty little plaything to use and discard."

I blink back tears, refusing to let him see how much his words hurt me.

"Kirill cares about me," I say defiantly, trying to hide my wavering voice. "He won't let you get away with this."

"Is that so?" Jurij smirks, releasing my chin and taking a step back. "We'll see about that."

"Where is he?" I demand, anger flaring up inside me.

The fear is still there, but I force it down, focusing on my loyalty to Kirill. I need to be strong for him, even if I don't know where he is or what's happening to him.

"Ah, so we're getting feisty now, are we?" Jurij chuckles darkly. He leans in close, his breath hot and rancid on my face. "Don't worry, sweetheart. He'll be here soon enough."

"Leave him alone!" I scream, trying to lunge at him despite my restraints.

"Enough! Know your place!" Jurij shouts, backhanding me across the face. The force of his blow sends my head snapping to the side, stars exploding in my vision. I taste blood, but I refuse to let him see how much he's hurting me.

"Take her to her room, I'm bored," Jurij orders to one of his men standing in the shadows. The man steps forward, grabbing me roughly by the arm and yanking me out of the chair.

I'm sure it will turn purple. That's not my biggest problem right now. My head's about to explode, it hurts so much from the punch.

"Please don't do this," I beg, trying to pull away from his iron grip. My body feels weak and heavy like I'm moving through molasses.

"Save your pleas for Kirill," Jurij sneers as the man drags me up the stairs and into a lavish bedroom. The contrast between the basement and this room is jarring – opulent wallpaper, plush carpet, and an enormous four-poster bed draped in silk curtains.

"Get on the bed," the man orders, shoving me forward. I stumble, catching myself on the edge of the mattress. My heart races in my chest, each beat echoing in my ears as I struggle to keep my breathing steady. I glance around the room, searching for any potential escape routes or weapons.

"Jurij said to make you comfortable," the man grunts, tossing a sheer silk nightgown at me. "Put this on."

"Go to hell," I spit, glaring at him with every ounce of defiance I can muster.

"Suit yourself," he shrugs, grabbing me by the throat and pressing me down onto the bed. Panic flares up inside me as I claw at his hand, trying to pry it away from my neck. Black spots dance in front of my eyes and my lungs scream for air.

"Stop!" I gasp, my voice barely a whisper. "I'll put it on."

"Smart girl," he says, releasing his grip and stepping back. My chest heaves as I suck in desperate breaths, trying to ignore the throbbing pain in my throat.

"Turn around," I command, struggling to maintain some semblance of control over this horrifying situation. He says nothing, just shakes his head with a cocky smile. I turn around.

It's humiliating, standing here in front of him while I slip the silky fabric over my head. The material clings to my body, leaving nothing to the imagination and I can feel his eyes on me, tracing every contour, every exposed inch of skin.

"Happy?" I snap, turning around to face him. He leers at me, his eyes raking up and down my body with undisguised lust.

"Very," he smirks, grabbing my arm once again and pushing me onto the bed. "Look at this. Now you really do look like a whore. A very expensive whore, which you are anyway." The silk sheets are cool against my skin, sending shivers down my spine. But I refuse to let him see how scared I am. I will not give him the satisfaction.

"Kirill will kill you for this," I hiss, glaring daggers at him as he towers over me.

"Then I guess we'll have to make sure he doesn't find out, won't we?" the man grins wickedly, reaching for the buttons on his shirt.

"Get away from her," a voice booms from the doorway, making both of us freeze in place. Another unknown man stands in the doorway. "She's just an Italian bitch. You can get better than her."

The man in front of me shrugs. "I was just having fun. I wouldn't let her near my dick anyway."

He goes outside and I hear the lock click.

I lie in bed for a long time, sleep avoids me.

I am too afraid.

And my face hurts like hell.

I know Kirill will come for me. I just have to hold on until then.

At some point, I drift into sleep, only to be jolted awake by the sound of the key turning in the lock. I sit up immediately and hold the blanket in front of me.

"Breakfast!" A new man hands me a bowl of porridge. He pays me no attention, simply hands it to me and walks out.

I grab the spoon, dip it into the porridge, but I don't have an appetite. With a sigh, I set it aside. Thoughts of escape, of finding a way out of this nightmare, consume my mind.

I don't know how much time passes, an hour or four, but sometime later Jurij reappears. He looks down at me, at the silk nightgown, and scowls. "I have no idea what he sees in you."

I pull up the covers, tense. Yesterday's asshole took my dress.

"Kirill..." I begin but Jurij interrupts.

"You think he's so much better than all of us, don't you? You think he deserves to be Pakhan... but let me enlighten you, sweetheart. This bastard you're so loyal to isn't even the rightful heir to the Diabol throne."

"What are you talking about?"

"You don't know, do you? I thought Luke was better than this. He, too, can't figure this out." he laughs darkly. "Vladimir wasn't his father. His mother had an affair with some pathetic bank officer."

"No," I roar, but Jurij doesn't back down.

"Vladimir found out and killed both of them in cold blood. Kirill shouldn't be Pakhan; it should've been me. And I will make sure everyone knows the truth, starting with you."

"Jurij, you're insane," I spit.

"Am I?" Jurij chuckles, his gaze fixed on me.

My heart sinks as I realize that Jurij might be telling the truth.

"He's nothing but a bastard. And soon, everyone will see him for the weak, spineless impostor he really is."

"Stop it!" I shout. I won't let him talk about Kirill like that. My husband, who has shown me kindness in this dark world we inhabit.

"He'll be nothing but a forgotten memory, a stain on the history of Diabol." Jurij laughs, stepping closer to me with a sinister glint in his eye. "With his death, I will claim what's mine."

"Never," I spit, glaring at Jurij with every ounce of hatred I possess. "Kirill won't die. He'll save me and kill you."

"Such loyalty," Jurij mocks, shaking his head.

"You're delusional if you think you can take over Diabol. The men will never follow you."

"Really?" Jurij retorts, a smug smile playing on his lips. "I've been talking to them, Emma. They want a true leader – someone who isn't afraid to embrace the darkness within us all."

"Darkness?" I whisper, my heart racing as fear surges through me. Could it be possible that Jurij has gained support from the other members of Diabol? Could he actually overthrow Kirill?

"Too late for Kirill," Jurij laughs, stepping back toward the door. "The wheels are already in motion, Emma."

Jurij went mad.

I'm quite sure of that.

He won't be able to beat Kirill.

Kirill.

I miss him so much.

"Kirill," I whisper, his name a lifeline as I close my eyes and imagine his face, his voice, the way he touched me. Like an oasis in this desert of fear, our memories together are my only solace. His deep, velvety voice that sent shivers down my spine; the warmth of his touch as he brushed a strand of hair away from my face, his fingers lingering on my cheek.

"Kirill," I say again, drawing strength from the memory of our love. I know he'll come for me. He has to. I refuse to believe that our connection is so easily severed by the cruel hands of fate.

"Please," I plead, tears streaming down my cheeks. "Find me."

"Talking to yourself, sweetheart?" The grating voice of one of my captors echoes through the door, and I flinch.

"Leave me alone!" I spit.

"Feisty, aren't you? I like that." His laugh sends shivers down my spine, but not the same kind Kirill's voice did.

"Leave me alone," I hiss, my heart pounding in my chest.

"Or what?" he taunts but not opening the door. "Kirill isn't here to save you."

I refuse to let him break me. I think of Kirill's touch, the way his fingers traced patterns on my skin as we lay entwined in each other's arms. The memory fuels a fire inside me that I didn't even know I possessed.

"Maybe not right now," I say, my voice steady despite the fear that grips me. "But he will be. And when he does, you'll wish you'd never laid hands on me."

"Is that so? But remember – your precious Kirill isn't here. You're all alone."

"Never," I whisper to myself. "I'm never alone. As long as I have my memories of Kirill, I'll always have some part of him with me."

I close my eyes again, letting the memory of our first night together wash over me, drowning out the cold and the fear. The way his strong arms wrapped around me, holding me close; how his kisses grew more heated, more urgent until I thought I might combust. How he'd whispered sweet words into my ear, words that promised protection and forever.

And with these memories come strength – the strength to endure, to hold on, to wait for Kirill to rescue me. Because I know that he will.

"Come for me, Kirill," I say softly, the words a prayer. "I'm waiting."

Chapter 11
Kirill

I sit in my chair, surrounded by my most trusted members. A heavy responsibility weighs on me as I consider the lives I'm placing at risk in this dangerous rescue mission. I cannot underestimate Jurij. He's an excellent strategist, he was my father's Consigliere for a reason.

The bastard.

But there's no turning back now; Emma must be saved.

"Alright, listen up," I command. "This operation is going to be unlike anything we've done before. We need to get in, retrieve my wife, unharmed."

Miloslaw, a man with sharp eyes, nods solemnly. His reputation as an infiltrator precedes him, and I know he's the best choice for blending into any environment. He speaks up, his voice low and calculated. "Do we have any intel on the inside? Security measures, guard rotations?"

"Natasha, what do you have?" I ask, turning to her. "Cameras and alarms are already taken care of. I'll monitor them remotely and keep you updated." She pauses, tapping at her laptop, then continues. "There are three main entrances, but I suggest using the service entrance in the back."

"Good work," I commend her, feeling a swell of pride. "Sergei, you're with me. We'll need your combat expertise if things go south."

"Of course, Kirill." Sergei, a tall, muscular man with a scar tracing the side of his face, nods in acceptance. I trust him implicitly, knowing his loyalty has never wavered throughout the years.

"Vlad, you and the others will provide backup and transport. Be ready to move on my signal." Vlad grunts an affirmation.

"Alright, now let's go over our escape routes," I say, spreading a detailed map across the table.

"Once we have Emma, I recommend taking this route here," Miloslaw suggests, tracing a line

"Natasha, any last-minute advice?" I ask, eager for the adrenaline-fueled rush.

"Stay sharp and stay focused. Remember that every second counts. I'll be watching your backs from here," she says, her eyes meeting mine for a moment before returning to her laptop.

"Let's do this," I declare.

This mission is personal, and I'll be damned if I let anything or anyone stand in my way.

As we make our final preparations, my thoughts drift to Emma, to the connection we share – dark, intense, and undeniably erotic. I can almost feel her soft skin beneath my fingertips, hear her breathy moans as we succumb to our most primal desires. The memory fuels my determination, stoking the fire within me. Emma is mine and no one touches what's mine.

"Ready?" Sergei asks, his voice steady and calm.

"More than ever," I reply.

"Then let's bring her home," he says, and with those words, we set out into the night, each of us aware of the risks and prepared to face whatever may come.

We approach the huge mansion, moving like shadows in the night. The darkness is our ally, concealing our movements from prying eyes. As we get closer, I can feel my heart pounding in my chest, a mixture of anticipation and anxiety. My thoughts return to Emma. I'm coming, moy dorogoy. I'm coming.

"Miloslaw, Sergei, take out the guards at the entrance," I whisper, keeping my voice low so it doesn't carry through the still air. I watch as they nod in understanding, their expressions focused and deadly.

"Vlad, you're with me. We'll cover them from here," I say, gesturing to a nearby vantage point that will allow us to provide support if needed.

As Miloslaw and Sergei make their way toward the unsuspecting guards, I can't help but admire their precision. They move with the grace and stealth of predators stalking their prey, their lethal intent apparent in every step.

"Remember, we leave no one alive," I remind them through our earpieces, my words met with curt acknowledgments. Everyone involved in this will be punished by death.

In a matter of seconds, the guards are neutralized, their still forms slumping to the ground without making a sound. It's impressive, but I know better than to let my guard down. This is just the beginning.

"Good work. Let's move," I command, leading the way inside the mansion. A narrow corridor stretches out before us.

"From here we split in two, " I instruct, watching as five team members disappear up the stairs. Each of them moves with purpose, their steps soundless.

"Stay in contact. If you find Emma, alert me immediately. And Jurij is mine." I add, my voice tense with urgency.

As I and the other four people press deeper into the house, we can sense the heightened alertness of the guards. With each passing moment, the realization that our presence has been discovered becomes more apparent. We encounter a group of guards blocking our path, their weapons raised and ready. The clash is immediate and intense. The air is filled with the sounds of gunfire and the unmistakable thud of bodies hitting the ground. The fight becomes chaotic; combined dance of fists, kicks, and weapons.

My muscles strain, fueled by determination and the unwavering desire to reach Emma. Every blow I deliver is swift and precise, aiming to incapacitate my opponents swiftly. The guards fight, unwilling to let us pass easily. We exchange blows, trading punches and dodging strikes with every ounce of skill we possess.

As the fight rages on, my team moves in perfect synchrony, covering each other's backs and providing support when needed. We communicate through brief gestures and instinctual understanding, a well-oiled machine working toward our common goal.

We take down guard after guard.

I hear a loud cry behind me. Looking back, I see that Kostya, a loyal young guy, reaching toward his heart. A dagger is sticking out of him.

I throw myself into the fight with renewed vigor. He was so young. He didn't deserve this.

As we take everyone out, I kneel beside my fallen comrade, his blood staining the ground. My hand trembles as I reach out to close his eyes, offering a final gesture of respect and gratitude. A knot forms in my throat, and a silent prayer escapes my lips, honoring his bravery and selflessness.

A mix of emotions swirls within me—grief, anger, and an unwavering determination. The loss fuels the fire within me, intensifying my resolve to protect who's mine.

Vlad approaches, his eyes filled with a mixture of sorrow and loyalty. He places a hand on my shoulder, a silent show of support.

"He fought bravely," I whisper, my voice barely above a hoarse murmur. "His sacrifice will not be forgotten."

Vlad nods, his grip on my shoulder tightening for a moment before releasing. We both know that we cannot dwell on our grief for long. There is still a mission to complete, lives to protect, and justice to be served.

I rise to my feet, my body aching with exhaustion but my spirit resolute. My eyes meet those of the surviving members of my team. We share a silent understanding—a promise to carry on, to fight for what is right, and to ensure that Emma's safety is secured.

Now we're splitting up one by one, and I'm turning to the right.

There is a long, dark corridor ahead of me.

Keeping my pistol ready, I open the door at the end of the corridor with a firm push.

I stay in the doorway, my heart pounding as I stare at Jurij's twisted, smirking face. He was about to leave through another door, his hand still on the doorknob.

The hatred boils inside me like molten lava, burning away any remaining vestiges of self-control.

"Jurij," I growl.

"Kirill," he sneers back, his eyes narrowing as he takes in my threatening stance. "Here to save your little princess?"

"The game is over, Jurij," I warn, my muscles tensing with each passing second.

"Or what?" he taunts, stepping closer to me, his breath hot on my face. "You don't have the guts."

"Try me." My voice is barely a whisper, but it's laced with venom. I put my gun away when I see he only has a knife. I hold out my hands. "Come on!"

Jurij lunges at me, his knife glinting in the light. With practiced ease, I dodge his attack and grab his wrist, twisting it until he drops the weapon. His eyes widen as I press my blade against his throat, my other hand gripping his collar, ready to strike the final blow.

"This was too easy. I expected better from you. Say goodbye, Jurij," I hiss, my voice cold as ice.

The fear in his eyes only fuels my hatred. He tries to speak, but the words are garbled, choked by the pressure of the blade on his throat. I tighten my grip, watching as blood begins to well around the edge of the knife.

"Please..." he gasps, the plea barely audible. But I have no mercy left for this man.

"Goodbye, Jurij." And with one swift, brutal motion, I slit his throat.

Blood spurts from the wound, staining my hands crimson, but I pay it no mind as I let his lifeless body crumple to the floor. The room falls silent, save for the pounding of my own heart.

It was too quick a death for him. That's not what I originally planned. I wanted him to beg, to cry.

But now I don't have time. I want Emma. She's more important than anything. I need to find her.

"Emma!" I shout, my voice echoing through the mansion.

"Kirill, we've found her!" Sergei's voice crackles through my earpiece, his words sending a jolt of adrenaline coursing through my veins.

"Where?" I demand, my heart racing as I await his response.

"Third floor, west wing. But there's a problem," he adds, his tone heavy with concern.

"Explain."

"Her captors rigged the room with explosives. If we try to force our way in, she'll be caught in the blast."

"Damn it," I mutter under my breath, my mind racing as I try to come up with a solution while I run the stairs two by two. "Miloslaw, can you disarm the explosives?"

"I'll need time," he replies, his voice steady despite the urgency of the situation.

"Then get started. And be careful," I say, knowing that one wrong move could mean disaster for all of us.

When I get there, Miloslaw is still working on disarming the explosives.

"Kirill, I'm ready!" he announces triumphantly.

"Good work. Now let's get Emma out of here," I say.

"Kirill," a weak, trembling voice calls from behind a locked door.

"Emma, hold on, I'm coming." I kick the door open, finally laying eyes on her.

She's huddled in the corner, her face battered and bruised, but alive. Relief floods through me, momentarily masking the anger that festers beneath the surface. She looks up at me with tear-filled eyes, and I can see the fear mixed with hope in her expression.

"Emma," I breathe, rushing to her side, my hands shaking as I gently touch her swollen cheek. "I'm so sorry."

"Kirill," she whispers, tears streaming down her bruised face. "You came for me."

"Always," I promise, pulling her into my arms.

"Kirill, we need to leave now!" Vlad says.

"Okay. Fire it all up!"

I hold Emma close, my emotions a tempestuous mix of relief, guilt, and desire, I know that the darkness within me has grown even deeper.

Chapter 12

Emma

My heart pounds in my chest.

Each beat echoes through my body like the drums of war.

I gasp for air.

My eyes snap open, and I'm no longer trapped in the damp cellar of my nightmares - but the memory lingers, chilling me to the bone.

"Emma," Kirill murmurs, his voice barely audible over the sound of my erratic breathing. His arms envelop me, the warmth of his body soothing the tremors that wrack my frame. "You're safe now. It was just a nightmare."

"Kirill," I choke out, tears streaming down my cheeks as I cling to him. The scent of his cologne - woodsy and masculine - wraps around me like a blanket, providing a sense of security I desperately crave.

"Shh, it's okay," he whispers into my ear, his breath warm on my skin. He strokes my hair, fingers gently combing through the tangles created by my restless sleep. "I'm here. You're not alone."

"Thank you."

The memory of my captivity still haunts me.

"Tell me what happened," he says, his voice firm yet gentle. "What did you see?"

"I...I was back in that place." My voice trembles, and I hate how weak I sound. I refuse to let my captors win, even if they continue to torment me from beyond the grave. "They were hurting me, Kirill. I couldn't escape."

"Those men will never touch you again," he vows, his grip tightening around me protectively. "I made sure of it."

"I know," I croak.

Despite the darkness that clings to him like a second skin, Kirill is my beacon - the light that guides me through the storm.

"Focus on my voice," he murmurs, pressing a tender kiss to my forehead. "Let it chase away the darkness."

"Your voice...it's like a lifeline," I admit. My heart hammers against my ribs, aching for the reassurance only he can provide.

"Then let me be your anchor," he replies. "I will hold you steady, Emma. You have nothing to fear."

"Promise?" I ask, needing to hear the words that tether me to this world, keeping the nightmare at bay.

"Always," he swears, his lips brushing against the shell of my ear. He cradles me close, shielding me from the ghosts that haunt our pasts. "You are safe with me, Emma. I won't let anyone hurt you again. And I've decided to assign some trusted members of my organization to provide additional security and protection for you. They'll be discreet, but they'll watch over you and ensure your safety."

"Okay," I say. The thought of having someone constantly watching over me should feel suffocating, but instead, it brings me a sense of peace. "Thank you," I whisper, feeling the heavy burden of my fears begin to lift. My breaths come easier now, the suffocating grip of terror gradually receding.

"Rest now," he urges, his fingers tracing soothing circles on my back. "I'll watch over you."

"Kirill," I say, reaching out to touch his face. "I love you."

"Love doesn't even begin to describe what I feel for you, Emma," he confesses, his eyes intense as they bore into mine. "You are my heart, my soul - everything that is good and pure in this world."

"Kiss me," I beg, needing to feel the all-consuming passion that ignites between us whenever our lips meet.

"Your wish is my command," he murmurs, claiming my mouth in a searing kiss that chases away the last vestiges of fear.

"Kirill," I whisper, feeling the need to share something important with him. "I have to tell you something."

"Anything, lyubeemaya," he murmurs, pressing a tender kiss to my temple.

"Your mother... I found out some information about her," I hesitate, unsure how he'll react to what I've uncovered. "She had an affair with a bank officer and your father... Vladimir, he killed them both. Your...Your father isn't Vladimir."

For a moment, Kirill just stares at me. But then, unexpectedly, he shrugs off the revelation as if it's inconsequential. "It doesn't matter, Emma. I barely remember my mother, and I was raised to be Pakhan. I'm the Pakhan."

"Doesn't it bother you?" I ask, searching his face for any hint of disturbance. "Jurij thought you shouldn't be Pakhan because of this."

"Jurij's opinion means nothing to me," he says firmly, his grip on me tightening protectively. "I am who I am, and no one can change that. You're the only one I truly care about, Emma. You're my family now."

"Kirill," I sigh, my heart swelling with affection for this man who has shown me such unwavering love and loyalty. "You are truly incredible."

He smirks, his eyes glinting with mischief. "Well, I do try."

As Kirill's fingertips graze my skin, goosebumps rise across my body. I can no longer deny the need that has been brewing between us. I want him to possess me completely – body and soul.

"Show me," I challenge, my voice breathy and eager. "Show me how possessive and passionate you can be."

"Emma," he growls, his eyes darkening with desire. "You have no idea what you've just unleashed."

"Make love to me," I whisper against his lips. "Please, Kirill."

"Emma," he groans, desire flaring in his eyes. "Are you sure?"

"Never been more certain of anything in my life," I admit, my hands tangling in his hair as I pull him closer.

"Then let me show you just how much I love you," he vows, his voice low and sultry.

Swiftly, his lips crash down on mine, and any lingering thoughts about past revelations are swept away by the tidal wave of passion that engulfs us. His hands roam my body possessively as if trying to claim every inch of me for himself.

"Mine," he whispers against my skin, his voice barely audible beneath the thundering of my heartbeat. "Say it, Emma. Say that you're mine."

"I'm yours, Kirill," I gasp, a shiver running down my spine at his fierce proclamation. "I belong to you, now and forever."

"Good," he murmurs, his fingers trailing down my spine until they reach the curve of my hips. "Then let me show you what it means to be mine."

He pulls me tightly against him, our bodies melding together in perfect harmony. As he explores me with a fervor bordering on madness, I feel myself spiraling further and further into the depths of pleasure.

"Kirill," I moan, clutching at his shoulders as the intensity of our connection threatens to shatter me.

"Emma," he growls in response, his own control teetering on the edge. "Hold onto me, Lyubimaya. Never let go."

I crave his touch like a drug, and I'm ready to surrender fully.

He starts by pressing gentle kisses on my neck and collarbone, the sensation making my pulse race. As his lips trail down my body, I arch my back in response, wanting more.

"God, you're beautiful," he murmurs, his eyes sweeping over every inch of me.

"Kirill," I breathe out, reaching for him as I blush under his intense gaze. "Please," I beg, desperate for his touch, my body tense with anticipation. He leans in, capturing my lips in a passionate kiss that steals my breath away. Our tongues dance together, savoring each other's taste.

He lowers himself onto me, his weight both comforting and electrifying. I can feel him hard against my thigh, and it sends shivers down my spine. He gently pushes my legs apart, positioning himself at my entrance.

"Ready?" he asks, his voice strained with desire. I nod, my heart pounding in my chest as he slowly pushes inside me.

He begins to move, each thrust sending sparks of ecstasy coursing through me. Our bodies move together in perfect harmony.

"Emma," he moans, his grip on my hips tightening. "You feel so incredible."

"Kirill," I whimper, the coil of pleasure tightening within me. He quickens his pace, his movements becoming more urgent as we both near our breaking point.

"Let go, Emma," he urges, his voice ragged with need. And with one final thrust, I shatter into a thousand pieces, the world around me dissolving into pure bliss. Kirill follows soon after, his body going rigid before collapsing onto me, both of us spent and breathless.

In Kirill's arms, I find solace and safety, and for now, that's enough.

Over the next few days, I begin to participate in activities alongside Kirill and his team. With Natasha's support, we start gathering evidence against those in the organization who supported Jurij. The process is slow and meticulous, but under Natasha's guidance, I find myself integrating back into their world.

"Alright, let's go over this again," Kirill says one evening, as he, Natasha, and I sit around a table littered with documents. "Who do we have confirmed as being involved with Jurij?"

"Based on the data we've collected so far," Natasha begins, scrolling through her tablet, "we have five individuals who were actively working with Jurij. Three of them are low-ranking members, while the other two hold more influential positions within the organization."

My stomach churns at the thought of traitors lurking among us, but I push the sickening feeling aside and focus on the task at hand.

"Okay, we can't afford to leave any loose ends," I say, taking a deep breath. "How want you to deal with them? Do you confront them directly or...?" I trail off, unsure of how to proceed.

Kirill leans back in his chair, his gaze thoughtful. "I don't want to get my hands dirty with them. They're not even worthy of my attention. Of course, their betrayal cannot go unpunished.

"What if we use a combination of techniques? Hacking their financial accounts, turning one of our enemies against them, and let them take them out one by one?" I ask.

"Sounds like a plan," Kirill says, stroking his chin. "You and Natasha take the lead on this operation."

I swallow hard, trying to keep my emotions in check. "We won't let you down."

As we work together over the following days, I feel a newfound sense of purpose and belonging.

The thought of being a part of something larger than myself is exhilarating, and I find myself growing closer not only to Kirill, but to everyone else on his team.

I understand this is just the beginning. We still have a long road ahead of us. But I know that no matter what challenges we face, we'll face them together.

Chapter 13
Kirill

I see my trusted Captains gather around my massive oak table. With a deep, measured breath, I lean forward, resting my elbows on the polished wood.

"Alright," I begin, my voice steady and commanding, "We need to establish new protocols and policies to ensure the safety and well-being of our members. We have many ideas to discuss tonight, but remember, everyone's input is valuable. Let's start with secure communication channels."

My father didn't care about anything but himself. He did not realize that the new times required modern answers. We need to be strengthened, not only externally but also internally.

I want a strong and invincible organization.

A strong future.

"Kirill," Natasha speaks up, "I've been working on an encrypted messaging app that would be exclusive to Diabol. It would allow us to communicate securely without the risk of outsiders hacking or intercepting our messages."

"Excellent work, Natasha," I praise, acknowledging her dedication.

"Thank you, Kirill. I can have a demo ready by next week for everyone to test out," she replies.

"Good. Next, let's talk about strategic response plans," I continue, scanning the faces of my men, looking for their insights.

"Boss," Magar, my other Enforcer, chimes in, "we should focus on training our members to respond to various situations quickly and efficiently. This includes improved surveillance, increased security at our properties, and rapid deployment of response teams when needed."

"Agreed," I nod, appreciating Magar's attention to detail. The safety of our organization is paramount, and it's essential to have skilled enforcers like him on the front lines.

"Let's also address emergency protocols," I add, my mind racing with the potential risks we face daily. "What measures do we have in place to protect our members and assets in case of an attack or other unforeseen circumstances?"

"Currently, we have a few safe houses scattered throughout the city, but they could be compromised if our enemies discover their locations," Ivan, our head of security, pipes up, his voice tinged with concern.

"Then let's establish more safe houses, and make sure their locations are known only to a select few," I decide, determined to minimize any vulnerabilities.

"Boss, I suggest we also invest in better security systems for our properties," Ivan continues. "We can install state-of-the-art surveillance cameras, bulletproof glass, and reinforced doors to deter any potential threats."

"Make it happen," I command, trusting Ivan's expertise.

Throughout the meeting, ideas flow freely as we brainstorm and analyze potential risks. The room is filled with passion and determination, everyone is focused on the common goal of strengthening Diabol and ensuring the safety of our members.

That's it.

This is what I want.

As the discussion winds down, my thoughts drift back to Emma. Her presence has both captivated and tormented me since I first saw her. I allow myself a brief moment to indulge in the thoughts of Emma. The way her laughter dances through the air like a delicate melody. The intoxicating scent of her perfume that lingers even after she's gone.

"Kirill, are you alright?" Natasha asks, pulling me from my thoughts. Her brow furrows with concern.

"Fine, just thinking about everything we discussed tonight," I lie. With a sigh, I stand and address my captains. "Thank you, all of you, for your input and dedication. Please ensure that these new policies are communicated effectively throughout the organization.

As the meeting ends, I watch them file out of the room and Emma enters.

My everything.

She sits in my lap and wraps her arm around my neck and holds my hand with the other. The warmth of her hand in mine sends a shiver up my spine.

"Kirill, I've been thinking about the training programs we discussed," Emma says softly. "We need to ensure that everyone has access to the best resources and instruction possible. From tactical combat techniques to digital skills – nothing can be left to chance."

I nod, squeezing her hand gently. "Agreed. If we want Diabol to be the best, we must provide our members with the tools they need to succeed."

"Exactly," she replies, a fiery passion burning in her eyes. "And it's not just about formal training, either. We should foster an environment that encourages innovation and collaboration. We could establish platforms for idea sharing and problem-solving, allowing every member to contribute their unique perspectives and talents."

Her enthusiasm is contagious.

It washes over me like a tidal wave, igniting a fire within me that drives me to push past the darkness that has haunted me for so long. I can't help but marvel at her strength and conviction. "Emma, that's brilliant. This inclusive culture will only serve to strengthen our organization, fueling creativity and camaraderie among our members."

"Let's start by identifying the key skills our members should master," Emma suggests, pulling up a holographic screen filled with potential training modules. "Tactical combat techniques, of course, but also digital security, intelligence gathering, diplomacy..."

"Interrogation techniques," I add, my mind already racing with possibilities. "And perhaps some courses on leadership and strategy, for those who aspire to take on more responsibility within the organization."

"Perfect," Emma agrees, her fingers flying across the screen as she compiles a list of potential instructors and resources. "We'll need to find the best experts in each field, people who can really inspire and challenge our members."

"Agreed," I say, watching her work with a mixture of awe and desire. The sight of her so focused, so driven, only serves to amplify the fire that burns within me. I yearn to taste the passion that fuels her – to savor its sweetness on my tongue, and drown myself in its intoxicating depths.

"Kirill?" Emma's voice pulls me from my thoughts, her concerned gaze searching my face for any sign of distress.

"Sorry," I murmur, forcing a smile onto my lips. "I'm just... really proud of what we're accomplishing here."

"Me too," she whispers, her hand reaching out to brush against mine. The touch is fleeting – barely more than a whisper of skin against skin – but it sends a jolt of electricity through my veins, igniting a hunger that threatens to consume me.

"Emma..." I begin, but then I change my mind. Now is not the time. Instead, I focus on the task at hand, channeling my desire into the work we have set before us.

Together, we continue refining our plans, shaping the future of Diabol with each decision we make. And as the hours slip by, I can't help but feel that we are building something truly remarkable – a legacy that will endure long after we are gone.

But beneath the pride and satisfaction, there lies a darker, more primal force.

A longing that refuses to be silenced, growing stronger with each stolen glance and lingering touch. It coils around my heart like a serpent, whispering seductive promises of pleasure and submission.

And as Emma and I work side by side, the fire that burns between us only grows hotter – a blaze that threatens to consume us both if left unchecked.

And in the depths of her eyes, I see the promise of a love that could burn hotter and brighter than any flame – if only we dare to reach for it.

JUDITH WHIMSEY

THE END

Acknowledgements

As always, there are so many people to thank for the contribution to this novel!

To my beta readers and to PHW Love, your guidance and enthusiasm on this novel were massivly valued. Thank you!

Robert, thanks for the support and encouragement.

And of course, my wonderfull family, my husband, children, Mum and Dad. There aren't enough words to say how important you are. Love you all!

About The Author

Judith Whimsey is from Hungary and lives in a lovely little town near the Danube. She likes dogs, cats and other cute animals. She is also fond of walks in the forest, rom-com movies, and any kind of songs that touch her for some reason. She has a husband and two children. She spends her little free time dreaming up sexy books.

PLEASE REVIEW THIS BOOK!

Review help authors more than you might think. If you enjoyed *The Price of Power* please consider leaving a review, it would be greatly appreciated by me.

SAY HELLO!

You can connect with Judith Whimsey in the following places:

Facebook: **https://www.facebook.com/judithwhimsey**
TikTok: https://www.tiktok.com/@authorjudithwhimsey
Mail: judithwhimsey@gmail.com
Web: https://judith-whimsey-plla79.mailerpage.io/

Gaby
I have to get married in order to repay a debt.
It' s the only way to save my father's life.
He will live, but I fall into the hands of a notorious mafia boss.
Can a monster be tamed?
Luke
You can't steal from me.
Everyone knows that.
Everything has a price, and sometimes that price is paid by the innocent.
I won't make any exceptions.

Sneak peek on the next pages.

The Price of Innocence

„We arrived too quickly at St Peter's Cathedral. When they opened the door, I thought of running away but realized it was pointless.

I straightened up and raised my head. I took a deep breath and slowly made my way towards my losing place.

I didn't want anyone to see the fear in my eyes. This obligation was a mockery of everything I've always believed in. It wasn't a tale of two lovers coming here to tie the knot in front of God and live happily ever after. I'm just a payment for something I didn't steal. How much is that debt? How much am I worth?

I felt my heart pounding as I walked between the benches to the rhythm of the music with my arms around my father. Everyone was standing and looking at me. A bunch of guests I didn't even know. I was grateful that my veil protected me from prying eyes and hid my nervousness. Savage – as everyone called him – stood at the altar waiting for me with patience. He looked better than anyone I'd imagined in my little-girl fantasies. Tall and fit. The dark tuxedo emphasized his muscular physique, exuding strength and sophistication. He looked like a rich businessman. His brown eyes never left me for a moment. His gaze revealed nothing, but penetrated deep into mine. As if he wanted to see my soul.

I took my place by his side. He reached out and I put my hand in his. It shivered a little, which of course, he noticed. He raised his left eyebrow and looked at me questioningly. I couldn't stand looking at him, so I turned my head towards the priest.

I couldn't comprehend anything at the ceremony. I said the lines automatically when I had to, and soon the thin gold ring is brightened on my finger. When the priest called for the first kiss, I turned towards him and waited. I was not aware that a tear escaped my eye until he gently wiped it away. He slowly leaned closer with open eyes, and our lips touched for a brief moment.

It's over. It is sealed. I've become the wife of the Savage.

He drove the car to the reception venue. This was the first time we were alone as husband and wife.

"What was that tear at the church?" he asked. I didn't stop staring out the window, so he continued, "What happened? Cat got your tongue?"

"Why did you marry me?" I couldn't hold myself back. It just came out.

"Are you expecting a love confession from me?" he asked defiantly.

"Of course not, but I'm curious." He looked at me, wondering what to say, but didn't answer. I became slightly irritated, because I didn't want to hear a long explanation. "Tell me the truth. I think I deserve it!"

"Really? What did you do to deserve it?"

I swallowed hard. I had to remind myself who was sitting next to me. "I know what my father did, and that's why we got married. But I don't understand what you have to gain from this. Wouldn't it be more logical to ask for your money back?"

He chuckled and said with a cynical smile, "How innocent you are! It will be fun to see what's left of it when I'm done!"

When he is done? I got scared again, but I had to know. "So, will you tell me then?"

"If you insist. You'll become a living example. A reminder of why it's a bad idea to screw me over. No one steals from me. If anybody tries, they will be punished. No second chances, no delay, no exceptions. Every wrong move has a price."

"I didn't do anything wrong," I whispered softly.

"You're right, and I'm very sorry. But your father loves you, and that's part of his punishment."

"Part of his punishment? So there's more?"

Other book from the Author

A young employee. A charming boss. A good dose of chemistry. And a deal.

Jenna Gold loves her job and feels like her life is on the right track. What she doesn't love are surprises, even if they come in a charming package like her new boss, Alexander Green.

Alexander is taking over his family's company but he doesn't expect to get a sexy assistant with it, Jenna Gold. While it's not wise to mix business and pleasure, sometimes you must bend the rules.

They make a deal. A month-long secret affair. No one can know. And there can be no extension. But sometimes contracts get broken.

Milton Keynes UK
Ingram Content Group UK Ltd.
UKHW010718140823
426838UK00001B/32